CW00350388

'Plass's greatest gift, in my opinion, is to weave the serious in with his playfulness in a way that doesn't seem forced and can be quite profound'
Sarah Hillman, *Church Times*

'Equal parts heart-warming as humorous and shows God's love for the mixed bag of people in a church'
Church of England Newspaper

'Plass handles the issue of how Christians relate to one another outside of their usual environment (church) with comedic skill and sensitivity. His characterisations are brilliant. I literally laughed out loud'
Christianity

Also by Adrian Plass from Hodder & Stoughton

The Sacred Diary of Adrian Plass: Adrian Plass and the
Church Weekend

The Shadow Doctor

Shadow Doctor: The Past Awaits

All Questions Great and Small: A Seriously Funny Book
by Adrian Plass and Jeff Lucas

STILL CRAZY

Love, laughter and tears from the
world of the Sacred Diarist

Adrian Plass

HODDER

First published in Great Britain in 2022 by Hodder & Stoughton Limited
An Hachette UK company

This paperback edition published in 2024

1

Copyright © Adrian Plass 2022

The right of Adrian Plass to be identified as the Author
of the Work has been asserted by him in accordance with
the Copyright, Designs and Patents Act 1988.

Unless indicated otherwise, Scripture quotations are taken from the *Holy
Bible, New International Version (Anglicised edition)*. Copyright © 1979,
1984, 2011 by Biblica Inc.® Used by permission. All rights reserved.

All rights reserved. No part of this publication may be reproduced, stored
in a retrieval system, or transmitted, in any form or by any means without
the prior written permission of the publisher, nor be otherwise circulated
in any form of binding or cover other than that in which it is published and
without a similar condition being imposed on the subsequent purchaser.

A CIP catalogue record for this title is available from the British Library

Paperback ISBN 978 1 473 67957 3
ebook ISBN 978 1 473 67955 9

Typeset in Sabon MT Pro by Hewer Text UK Ltd, Edinburgh
Printed and bound in Great Britain by Clays Ltd, Elcograf S.p.A.

Hodder & Stoughton policy is to use papers that are natural, renewable
and recyclable products and made from wood grown in sustainable
forests. The logging and manufacturing processes are expected to
conform to the environmental regulations of the country of origin.

Hodder & Stoughton Limited
Carmelite House
50 Victoria Embankment
London EC4Y 0DZ

www.hodderfaith.com

This book is dedicated to Ken and Liz, partners and friends through pleasure, pain and the odd pandemic. Also to our wonderful community in West Auckland Vineyard Church for continuing to be a real church through such difficult times.

Contents

Introduction

Still Crazy. So, as far as this book is concerned, who exactly is still crazy? I'll mention the important candidate in a minute. The other one is me. Many are crazy enough to follow any path that might lead to a scent or sight of God, but the way I am made might add intensity to the pursuit. What do I mean by that? My explanation has to begin with a rather bizarre confession.

I have always rather enjoyed balancing things on my head. Perhaps 'enjoyed' is not quite the word. Over the years I have become increasingly interested in discovering just how far I might be able to go in terms of weight, height and variety of balanced objects.

What kinds of things do I balance? The list is long and still growing. It includes plates; bowls; chairs; pets (moderate success); upside-down coffee tables; fragile ornaments (least popular, but generates the highest grade of agitated response from onlookers); large, heavy reference books in towers of variable height; bottles; planks and giant flowerpots.

Why do I do it? Apart from the irresistible drive towards ever-increasing height and weight, a clue lies in that reference to fragile ornaments. There is an obscure pleasure to be found in shocking and perhaps slightly disturbing those who unsuspectingly enter a room to find me engaged in an activity that is silent, bizarre, unnaturally still and possibly on the very cusp of disaster.

However, there came a day when Bridget, my wife, walked into the lounge and proceeded to speak to me for two or three minutes without seeming to register the fact that an upturned three-legged French milking stool was precariously poised on the centre of my head.

She maintained it was because she had become so accustomed to my strange behaviour that the odd French milking stool was hardly worth a mention.

I thought about this and realised that I would have to go for gold.

A few mornings later, when I knew that Bridget was coming to the end of a radio programme she was listening to in the sitting room, I sat on a stool in the kitchen with a ridiculously huge china plate balanced on my head. In the centre of the plate stood an uncorked bottle that was three-quarters filled with red wine.

Anyone who has been brave or stupid enough to try something like this will know that the margin for error in these circumstances is probably too infinitesimal to be measured. After locating the exact balancing point for my plate and bottle it was necessary to keep my body perfectly still as I began the terrifying process of lowering both hands, millimetre by millimetre, down onto my lap.

After that it was essential to remain committedly statuesque until Bridget appeared.

Minutes passed. I was just beginning to wonder how long I could survive without moving or taking a deep breath, when, out of the corner of my eye, I noticed a slight movement in the direction of the window that overlooked

2

our garden. Summoning every ounce of self-control, I revolved the top half of my body, inch by hard-won inch, until I was facing the garden.

A man was watching me through the window, a tape measure dangling from one hand, his face frozen into a state of utter incomprehension. I knew him. He was called Tim, and we had arranged for him to come round that day to measure up for some repair work that needed doing to our shed.

Tim and I stared silently through the glass at each other for what felt like half an hour, but must have only been a matter of seconds, before he abruptly turned away and began to measure with minute concentration a part of the shed that needed no repair.

My relationship with Tim changed forever. That engagement of our eyes was never discussed, but every time we met I seemed to see, etched into the very structure of his honest face, a question that could not be easily asked or satisfactorily answered.

'Why were you sitting completely still on your own in the kitchen with a huge plate and an open bottle of wine balanced on your head?'

Tim would not, of course, have been alone in hunting for a way to ask that question. He and Bridget could have had quite a lively conversation on the subject.

There are two reasons for including this account. First, it is true. Second, it does epitomise a part of the way I am made, an off-centre perspective that applies to faith, writing, public speaking and private conversation. If we were talking about driving, I might describe it as an intense desire to explore the strange, funny, puzzlingly pointless little side turnings that, generally speaking, we are too busy to bother with.

My second candidate for the label of 'crazy' would be – God. I would suggest, with the profound humility for which I am so commonly admired, that Jesus was afflicted (or I should say blessed) with the same kind of off-centre perspective in his storytelling and in his dealings with individuals and groups. Standing ideas on their heads, taking an unexpected direction that had not occurred to anyone before, refusing to be confined by others' assumptions and guesses that have congealed into false facts: all of those are tendencies and talents that I could never match, but can at least aspire to.

Those who really love the Church, and probably those who do not, would find it difficult to argue with the contention that a radical change of perspective is needed. Does one have to actually be crazy to attempt such a task? Strictly speaking, no, but I can testify to the fact that the process of tackling it is likely to attract some puzzled looks along the way.

There are always new, and occasionally startling, things to be discovered. Bridget recently pointed out that the first few words of John 3:16, probably the most familiar verse in the New Testament, must be addressed to the unredeemed world. Seems obvious, doesn't it? Or maybe not.

As I was looking through the rest of the verse with that thought in mind, something else struck me. You can work through the argument of this for yourself, but it occurred to me that if Jesus was capable of giving in to temptation (and I would suggest that everything loses meaning if he was not), then God did not just *give* his only begotten Son, he *risked* him.

Good luck wrestling with the cosmic logic of this fact, but that is how it looks to me. I tried to catch my fluttering response to this discovery so that I could put it in a cage made of words. You could call it a poem. This is how it went. Still a work in progress, but the feeling is there.

The John 3:16 Verse We All Think We Know

You so loved the world,
Not the saved world,
Not the good world,
Not the bad world,
Definitely not the only sect that will ever get into heaven,
Absolutely not the sect that will only ever reach heaven
    by the excessive grace of yours truly,
Not the clothed world,
Not the naked world,
Not the hungry world,
Not the planet of the fatties.

No, the world that you loved, just as it was,
Is still the world that you love,
Just as it is,
Just as we are.
It is me,
Just as I am.
You so loved (thus revealing a sad lack of taste for one so
    creative) this vast collection of misshapen vegetables,
Including, incidentally, those among us who are deeply,
    deeply ashamed, and should be,

5

Including also, for certain sure, those among us who are
    deeply, deeply ashamed and really should not be,
So, so loved us,
So, so love us,
That you gave and continue to give whatever it takes to
    keep as many as possible trudging happily or mutter-
    ing worriedly along with you towards forever.

To be honest, at this point understanding can grind to a
    creaky halt,
But my heart does not do that.
My heart continues to walk on like a rain-soaked
    Liverpool footballer,
Because I think I am just beginning to get it now.
You loved the entire unredeemed world so much
That you were crazy enough to risk your only beloved
    Son.
You risked him.
Risked.
I had not realised that.
Forgive me.
I realise it now.
Thank you.
Thank you very much indeed.

And so, I invite you to join me on this journey along undis-
covered paths and forgotten byways, in the search for one
place, one thing, one person.

    Lots of laughs along the way. A few tears. It can feel a bit
reckless, but risk appears to be within the character of God.
We will get there.

Still Got Something to Say

Our whole family loved The Traveling Wilburys. We took their first album on holiday with us when our kids were younger and we all got to know the songs pretty much by heart. It wasn't until many years later that a bit of one of the tracks became a slightly annoying earworm: '. . . even if you're old and grey . . . you still got something to say'.[1] Those two snippets triggered a defensive petulance. I know why. I was coming up to the age of seventy and, although parts of my body were beginning to show signs of wear, I was enjoying all the creative stuff as much as or more than ever. Simply thinking and dreaming has always been one of my favourite hobbies. Accepting and sharing that fact has been very good for me. As to the value of the stuff I produced as a result of all this churning – well, who knows?

Why on earth would I not still have something to say when I'm old and grey? For goodness' sake! Don't you dare patronise me with your suggestion that, as I sit gibbering in the corner, there might be a slim chance of some tiny aspect of my inane drivel proving to be very nearly worth listening to. Let's just get this straight . . .!

I can be very childish at times, but I am slowly maturing. Old age may be upon Bridget and me, but we have no

---

[1] 'End of the Line' by The Traveling Wilburys, from the album *The Traveling Wilburys Volume 1*, 1989.

intention of going gently. In fact, we have rather a lot to say. Well, I do anyway, but increasingly things seem to happen to prevent me from sharing my wonderful words of faith and wisdom. Here is an example.

Floods and Following Jesus

One morning Bridget and I agreed that I would settle down to write a letter for my website. It was a good day to choose, because she was due to begin a new voluntary role at our church café in the morning, and I had none of those niggling loose ends to deal with at home. At ten o'clock I sat down at the table in my sitting-room, lifted the lid of my laptop, opened a new file and took a sip of my coffee. There was no clear reason to believe that my work would be postponed or interrupted.

You know, I am sure that God would say he allows me quite a lot of slack. But I do the same for him. I really do. I am prepared – if not exactly happy – to temporarily shelve such issues as predestination and free will, all the human suffering that is allowed by an omniscient and all-loving creator, and, as the writer of 1 John said, and as we seem to see playing out on the world stage as I write, the devil being allowed to rule the world.

Anyway, you would think, would you not, that the Almighty might have rewarded my patient forbearance over these issues by sending an experienced angel in to ensure that I could get some work done that morning? All I can say is that the one dumped on me must have been on divine work experience. I had typed just two words when disaster happened.

On the other side of the table at which I was sitting stood a very tall, fluted glass container filled with fresh flowers. A moment earlier there had been a lot of water in it. Suddenly there was none. Maybe I nudged the table leg with my knee. Whatever the reason, this vase suddenly slipped from the china coaster it was standing on and fell heavily across the table in my direction. The glass did not actually break, but the water flowed out and across the wooden surface like a freak wave. Objects lying around on the table became small islands in a sea of stale, flower-fragmented, stained water.

Panic-stricken, I immediately rescued my laptop then rushed to the kitchen as fast as three score years and ten would allow and collected what was left of our last giant kitchen roll (I love those giant kitchen rolls). Seconds later I liberated and frantically mopped my mobile phone before anything else, closely followed by some printed sheets of paper, a pink plastic box of computer sticks and my new black spectacle case. The water remained. There was a lot of it. No exaggeration. There was a lot.

Repeated applications of paper towels barely touched the problem. Not only that, but as I had nothing handy in which to dump the sodden lumps of tissue, they simply remained on the table, slowly, maddeningly releasing the water that they were supposed to have absorbed for good. Saying some quite bad things, I staggered back to the kitchen for a receptacle.

A few minutes later, after feverish activity, the kitchen roll was exhausted, and the results formed a strange misshapen mass in a big china bowl.

One problem. The table was still awash.

Only one resource remained. Not for the first time I cursed the fact that we have no downstairs toilet. Martyrdom is always a possibility in the committed Christian life, but I don't see why we should have to put up with trudging repeatedly up and down stairs before it happens.

It worked, though. Toilet paper eventually did the trick. Half a roll or more it needed before that expanse of polished wood was totally dry once more. Sitting beside the bowl, now piled ridiculously high with a mountain of soaked, dripping tissue, I breathed a weary gasp of relief. Back to square one.

At that precise moment – the house phone rang.

For a moment I teetered on the brink of Basil Fawlty mode. But it was all right. The call brought good news from someone I really like. Perhaps my flood incident, annoying though it was, highlights the fact that however carefully we plan, we can never be completely in charge of what happens next – which happens to be more or less the subject I had intended to write about.

Bridget and I are now absolutely clear about one aspect of this strange business of trying to be followers of Jesus. No matter how carefully, committedly and prayerfully we plan our lives, it is almost impossible to know what God is doing, or what our contribution to his work is likely to be. In the past this depressed and annoyed us at times. Perhaps we wanted to be driving and controlling the process of living as a Christian, whatever that might actually mean. Nowadays, we still ask continual questions about what is going on and how we might be allowed to fit in, but there is a profound and growing sense of liberation accompanying a decision to let God be in charge, especially as more interesting and unexpected things seem to happen when he picks up the reins. We've been telling people God is in charge of our lives for years, and almost managing to believe it, so it is probably about time it became true.

Just one more thing to get off my chest. I've been cheered and encouraged by the total commitment with which representatives of the Christian Church vividly reflect and live out one of the commands given by Jesus in the thirteenth chapter of John's Gospel. It goes like this:

> *A new command I give you: bully, mistreat and neglect one another. As I have bullied, mistreated and neglected you, so you must bully, mistreat and neglect one another.*

OK, I might have got that slightly wrong, but the fact is that we have recently met quite a lot of Christians who are wrestling with hurt and bewilderment because they have been marginalised or oppressed or manipulated by people who were supposed to be their brothers and sisters.

One of the really tricky issues is that in many cases the people who caused such hurt may have done so with the best of intentions. It is easy for us to race excitedly ahead with visions that spring from human optimism and plans that have been agreed by everyone except the Holy Spirit, but if we take a moment to look behind us we may see bodies on the road. I'm quite sure I've been guilty of this myself. Thank goodness God has organised such a warm and efficient means of bringing light into the darkness.

God is very nice, if extremely difficult to read, and he's looking for people to join him behind the counter. As the years go by, we are pretty sure only one qualification is required. Willingness to be there and to do what we're told.

There you are. I dealt with the flood, dried the table, controlled my bad language and wrote the stuff that I had more or less planned. A peace descended. I did my best not to worry about that.

What of Me?

Now that we have reached these advanced years, we occasionally sense polite young people restraining their curiosity about what could possibly make it worthwhile for us to get up in the morning. Some are not so polite.

I remember being on a bus many years ago, when I was a rosy-cheeked young man in my very early fifties. There were only two other people travelling on this comfortably solid lump of late-twentieth-century public transport. They were on the double seat facing me. One was a rather sulky-looking slab of a youth whom I judged to be nineteen or twenty years old. Squashed in next to him was an attractive girl of about the same age. She was clearly with the youth in a specifically geographical sense, but the hunted expression in her eyes and a succession of what looked to me like escape rehearsal twitches in her body suggested that, at the very least, she was contemplating the joyful prospect of elsewhere.

After a few minutes of moribund silence, the youth must have decided that the time had come to resurrect himself enough to favour the other occupant of his small world with a shaft of dazzling wit. He raised his head.

'If I wuz to wake up tomorrer,' he said, with lugubrious intensity, 'and found I was fifty, joo know wot I'd do?'

Pushing her hair away from her face, and her face away from his, she replied dispassionately, 'No, I don't. What would you do?'

'I'd top myself.'

The girl turned to stare at him for a moment. Was there a more animated expression on her face? Was it mingled with an expression of yearning? I thought I could guess what she was thinking, and even the words she might have refrained from uttering . . .

'I wish you were fifty.'

Harsh, if I was correct, but I did empathise with her, and I should admit that I did have some sympathy with that young man's perspective. I might not have expressed my opinion as bluntly in a public place in the hearing of someone who showed all the signs of having already toppled into the hellish abyss of fifty-year-old hopelessness and despair, but I do recall having, at the same point in my fifties, a very agnostic attitude to any possible quality of life after the age of seventy. Now that I am past my seventy-third birthday, I am, as I have said, finding much to enjoy, thank you very much.

Take tea, for instance. We love tea. Before I go any further, let me make it absolutely clear that I am not talking about the apparently ubiquitous belief that most problems encountered by the elderly can be solved with a cup of tea, and just about all of them with the addition of a biscuit. That is not the case.

Tea is one of God's greatest and most enduring creations, and he did quite well with biscuits. Bridget and I have always relished those things. Over the years, tea has saved our sanity and almost our lives on a number of occasions. OK, gin and tonic in proper glasses with slices of lemon and lime, or Lagavulin whisky entirely on its own might also do the trick, but those who, like that member of The Traveling Wilburys I did not specify, become a little patronising towards us mature specimens, are unlikely to start sloshing that sort of stuff around just to keep us socially sedated.

Yes, tea is an ongoing miracle, but miracle is only coincidentally an anagram of reclaim. The time has to be right, and we, in cooperation with God, will choose the time. Thank you.

One sad fact that cannot be miracled away by even the best tea and biscuits as we reach this age is the relatively frequent death of contemporaries and, even more alarmingly, friends, family and people in the news who are several years younger than us. Embracing death is a strange business, an anticipated and inevitable shock that comes rolling into the terminus. I don't like it.

Some claim to be unmoved by the prospect of death. I am not. I do not wish to die. I wish to remain alive. Once or twice in my life, friends who are not Christians have made comments like this: 'Of course, you Christians won't have any problem about dying, will you? You're just looking forward to moving on into glory or heaven, or whatever you call it.'

One particular friend was frankly sceptical when I pointed out that, by the time he was in Gethsemane, Jesus was clearly dreading the ghastly events that were still to come. In fact, he said, 'My grief is so great that it almost crushes me.' He also asked, if it was possible, to be allowed to back out of the whole crucifixion nightmare. If anyone should have been able to picture the 'glory', it was him.

My friend was puzzled. He said that he knew the Bible well and remembered none of this. He would go and check it out. I still don't know if he did or not.

A surprising number of believers and most unbelievers find it almost impossible to get their heads round one statement that sounds simple but is eternally not.

He became man.

Jesus the man knew all the weaknesses and strengths and joys and tragedies of being a real man. In a way that is in most respects inexplicable to us, he also knew exactly the same experiences of being the real God who was inhabiting the real man.

Clear as mud, eh? But that's where it's at. And that's why he was conflicted. And that's why we are as well. We inherit the burden and the blessing. Choice in that respect does not appear in the contract.

As a very limited man I cannot imagine how I would ever face past, present or future without the Spirit that seems to be in me. I am profoundly interested in heaven, whatever that turns out to be, as long as it doesn't involve singing 'Shine Jesus Shine' for the next ten million years. At the same time, I love this world and my life, and I want to hang on to it for as long as is humanly (or spiritually) possible. Something like that.

Here is a poem I wrote years ago, when I was ambitiously asking myself how the combination of man and God worked itself out in the consciousness of the human being called Jesus. It is called 'What of Me?'

Yes, he will rise again.
But what of me?
Though death flaps down to take me like a huge black
    bird
Casting ragged shadows over lilies of the valley,
Over milky moonlit seas,
Sunrise glory,
Sunset flame,
Peach and pearl in Galilean skies,
The coolness of a woman's hand,
Children's eyes,
The rasp of rough-grained wood against the skin,
Light in the gaze of men, who, by a miracle of faith, have
    seen,
Heard, walked, talked,
Discovered that their pitted skin is whole and clean.
Sabbath walks, meandering through rolling fields of wheat;
The chattering and chuckling of my friends,
Their sweet naivety.
A scent of cooking fish,
The call to eat;
Old stories by the fire;
Good wine;
A kiss;
Love and wisdom in my mother's smile;
The tears of those who loved me much
Because I gently, fiercely took away their sin.
And will I rise again?
Indeed, the Son of Man must rise and live once more.
But what of me?
What of me?

I Don't Remember It That Well

There's nothing funny about serious loss of memory as we get older. Bridget's dad (and therefore her mum as a consequence) suffered from the onset of severe dementia in his final years. Bridget and I are not yet afflicted in that way, but we do have the most ridiculous conversations several times each week that pursue a tortuously twisting trail of failed memory as we move inevitably towards the point where we can't recall what we were trying to call to mind in the first place. We thought we would like to give you a flavour of these time-wasting verbal excursions, so here is one.

A: Who were you talking to on the phone earlier?

B: What? Oh, it was – oh, no! The name's gone! The girl from – you know – that place. The place. The place. The place before – wherever it was.

A: You mean the place before Bromley?

B: No, no! The place before that. Where we had the – *you* know – where we had to put up with all the—

A: Oooh!! You mean the girl we always said looks like – who's the woman we liked and then we didn't because she – oh, what did she do? She did something. It was in all the papers. You must remember. She was on that programme.

B: Which programme?

A: Oh, come on! You know – the programme. The programme with the bit at the beginning set in – where was it? Not Blackpool. The other one.

B: Oh, yes! The place where we stopped off that wet afternoon to watch – oh, for goodness' sake! The film with that bloke – tall, something wrong with his left leg. You

always thought he looked exactly like the manager of
– aaah!

A: No, hold on, you're thinking of – thingy.

B: Thingy?

A: Friend of your dad's. Old friend of your dad's. Drove a
– you know – great big whatsit – great big thing.

B: Ah! Lived in – hold on a minute. Two streets away from
yours – big wide road with—

A: Yes! King – King something Street – same name as your old
friend's brother's solicitor. Come on! You know who I'm
talking about! Thin, serious, got a – thing on his face.
Never wanted to eat on Mondays. N-o-o-o, it's gone.

Pause.

A: Who *were* you talking to on the phone just now?

B: What? Oh, I haven't got the faintest idea.

Waiting for God?

*Contrasting imperatives are showered over Christians like
confetti at a divorce. We must rest; we must work sacrificially.
We should not doubt, but doubt is an essential aspect of faith.
Humility is good, but it can be a poor relative of pride. We
are free in Christ, but we can't do this, or that, or anything
remotely bordering on what I just saw you doing. Heaven is
definitely not up there in the sky above us, but we're pretty
sure we know it's not in the Pacific Ocean just south of New
Zealand, so where on earth is it? We must accept that Adam
and Eve were real, living people, but only in a mythical sense.
The good news is that nothing can separate us from the love
of God in Christ; the bad news is that it doesn't apply if we're
goats, in which case eternity is looking bleak.*

Of course, we all know that reality is seldom simple. Two or three or even more things can quite legitimately be true and apparently in conflict with each other at the same time. That is what makes life and faith and the person of Jesus fascinating, and it is also the reason why we have to be careful and caring as we separate and offer to others the tangled threads of how things really are.

Get moving and work hard, but make sure you wait for God? There's another choice between false opposites.

I've been tangled up with the whole Christian thing for many years now. A lot of things fascinate me as I look back over those years. One concerns the business of having a relationship with God.

In the days when I was embarking on this weird journey of faith, there was a clear and very far from unspoken assumption that a rich and satisfying familial closeness to God began at some point on day one and would continue for the rest of my life. I wanted that to be the case, and I certainly proclaimed loudly that it was the case, but actually it was not. Of course, I can only speak for myself, but I know now that I was and am a work in progress, and that in the beginning I was probably incapable of even beginning to understand what I had got myself into.

Over the years I was sustained by a profound hope that the same unconditional 'Yes' offered to a thief on a cross had been offered to me by this Jesus, who, as far as that lost sixteen-year-old could tell, might really have the power to make impossible dreams come true.

That hope is the hand that God has stubbornly held on to over my lifetime, but thirty-six years ago there was a gear change. It began with the shock of learning, in the middle of abject failure, that God is nice, and he likes me. The liking is important. Do you want a relationship that only consists of someone loving you, despite the fact that they can see nothing likeable about you? That's not a real relationship, is it? That's not an exchange of smiles and jokes and a few tears. There are no layers in it. Not a lot of fun. And although I loathe a certain variety of 'fun' because it often lacks humour – well, it has to be *available* at least, don't you think?

One or two people have challenged me on my contention that God is 'nice'. The word is too pale, they say. Too thin. Surely God is much, much more than that. Surely our respect and gratitude for what he has done demand that we speak about him in terms of reverence and awe. Well, sometimes that will be appropriate, but as I discover just how charming God is, and how ingeniously he has worked on my behalf, I find myself wanting to say to people, from my heart, 'You know, you'll really like him, he's so nice.'

Over the last ten years, the creator of the universe has been very kind to me. There have been changes in my life and in my understanding of myself that I would not have believed possible. There is also a new and really quite exciting, if tentative, perception of the way in which the Holy Spirit does stuff in this world when we stop offering what we haven't got and agree to be part of plans that we have not initiated, even when that process leaves us feeling a little (or very) diminished. Believe me, that diminution is almost certain to happen from time to time.

Bridget and I were speakers at a weekend conference a while ago. On the Friday evening we introduced ourselves and said a few things to get the weekend going, but by the time we got into bed that night I was feeling less than optimistic about the rest of the weekend. This is not unusual, I hasten to add. In the years when I was even more up myself than I am now, I was much more confident. People always love to laugh, and that was my thing. Not too difficult if it's your thing. Over the last few years, Bridget and I have operated in a mode that is closer to teaching and inspiration than performance, although we still try to have lots of laughs with the groups we address. The burden for us, now that we genuinely care about getting out of God's way so that people can be helped, is that it means he is in charge, and although we plan carefully, we are never quite sure what he is going to do.

On that Friday night I asked God to give me a dream to help with the rest of the conference. Did he answer my prayer? Who can say for certain? All I can say is that in my dreams that night, three different people all clearly said the same word.

Disappointment.

What I do know for sure is that, after I mentioned this on the Saturday morning, a number of people came to us asking for prayer in connection with that specific problem.

Truth is, there's a lot of it about. Disappointment, I mean. I know I am not the only one who has wondered why the extravagant promises of conversion never quite materialised. It works fine for some people. Like putting on a new coat. Slip it on and off you go. Well, bully for them. All I am saying is – don't give up. I am so enjoying the beginnings of something that feels like a real relationship with God. It is a fondness. It is more than a fondness. It has taken so long to develop. Sometimes it is fragile, and I become fearful. Every now and then it is strong, particularly when I don't analyse it too much.

Remember this. There is only one testimony worth presenting to the world. It is, quite simply, the truth. Wherever we are, whatever is happening or not happening, however much or little our experience matches that of others, no matter which point we occupy on the spectrum between misery and joy, we need to speak it out, and wait for love to awaken us and nurture us and teach us what a relationship with God might really mean.

Quick-fire Interview

Every now and then I am asked to contribute to a magazine article that combines offerings from a few writers, all under the same heading. One of these was described as a 'quick-fire interview'. Brief questions inviting brief answers. I know that when I was younger I would have spent some time cogitating over tasks like these. Nowadays I don't seem to employ many filters at all with questions like this. This is what I wrote, slightly updated so that it does at least seem to make sense. You may, of course, disagree.

Describe yourself in three words.
Good, bad, ugly.

What is the trait you most deplore in yourself?
Overuse of my talent for self-effacement.

What is the biggest misconception people have about you?
That I enjoy a certain hideous variety of fun. I humbly confess that I would probably kill any living thing to avoid that sort of fun.

What's the meaning of life?
Evidence suggests that the hokey-cokey is almost certainly what it's all about, but it is terribly easy to put a foot wrong.

High church or low church?
Any height at which spontaneity is not carefully organised.

What would you do if you were the Archbishop of Canterbury for the day?
Take a day off.

What did you want to be when you were growing up?
Grown up. And married to Hayley Mills.

What's the worst job you've ever done?
The only real one that springs to mind is working in a meat factory when I was just sixteen. Ghastly for a number of unrepeatable reasons. Don't ask. Leaving those searing memories behind, let's move on to some silly job jokes.

Postcard factory. Nothing to write home about. Working for a kidnap gang. They had to let me go after a fortnight. Sewerage work. Seemed like one of the big jobs, but after a while I was just going through the motions.

What would you be doing now if you weren't a Christian?
Becoming slightly perturbed about the fact that I'm biblically dead.

How do you take your tea?
In England.

Tell us a secret . . .
There is a slim but healthy chance that there might actually be a God.

Where are you going for your next holiday?
Not sure yet. Possibly the spare bedroom. Could be the shed. Besides, Bridget and I don't do holidays. We do recreational outreach – bit tricky in our shed. (At the time of writing, the pandemic still ruled.)

What was the last film you watched?
A screen musical about a young couple who meet in a swimming pool water flume and want to marry but discover that their families disapprove of the relationship. It was called *Wet Slide Story*. We are now planning to see a new film about an elderly, hairy man who runs around naked, claiming to be an Old Testament prophet. It's called *A Streaker Named Isaiah*.

What has been your biggest disappointment in life?
Having a tattoo done on my seventieth birthday and finding that nobody objected . . .

What do you consider your greatest achievement?
Writing the two *Shadow Doctor* books, giving up smoking thirty years ago, and teaching my daughter to like olives and whisky.

Insurance

Now there is nothing wrong with funeral insurance plans, and absolutely nothing funny about the death of people we love. Recent times have been drenched with sadness as the coronavirus has decimated families all over the world. One thing that does disturb us is the way that advertisements for funeral cover (in this country, at least) encourage an absurd notion that the whole death thing can be leapfrogged over and family sadness dispelled with the promise of enough cash to pay for the funeral, and a trivial gift awarded just for 'signing up'.

Perhaps Jesus would have attracted more followers if he had been armed with a load of gift cards from a certain high-street chain: 'This is not just salvation – this is M&S salvation.'

GEORGE: (*a repellently lively looking elderly man who is cutting a massive sandwich with enormous energy, greets his guest brightly*) Hello there, Jean from next door. Come to get your parsnip pan back?

JEAN: (*equally brightly*) That's right, a little treat. We're having parsnips again tonight.

G: Yum! Family OK? Norman? Benny and Jenny? And the other one? The little fat one, who blows bubbles a lot and has to be burped three times every hour?

J: Oh, Uncle Keith. He's fine. So what are you up to, George who lives here? You're looking very merry and bright, if you don't mind me saying so!

G: Me? Oh, yes! I'm having a grand time! I've just made one of my little sandwiches and I've spent the last hour or so planning my death! I've already signed up for one of those funeral plan insurance agreements.

J: Ooh! Aren't you the multi-tasker! Funeral plan, eh? What fun!

G: (*points at pamphlet*) Yes, take a look at this. See, right on the top of the pamphlet it says, 'Sign up with us and your funeral worries will be dead and buried.'

J: (*seriously impressed*) I like that! I really like that, George! George, do you think this firm would suit me? In the past I've always worried that funeral people might be a bit – you know – insensitive?

G: Not these people, Jean. Here, you read this out!

J: (*reads with huge interest*)

By signing up here, you'll say goodbye to fear,
Where kicking the bucket's concerned.
As you hit the deck, we'll be writing a cheque,
For your corpse to be buried or burned.
They chuckle delightedly together.

J: Isn't that lovely? A lovely light but caring touch! Really makes you almost feel you'd *like* to die.

G: Do you know, that's exactly how I feel! I *want* to die. I'd like to die – right now if I could. Really looking forward to it. I tell you what, Jean from next door, this really is a wonderful insurance plan.

J: I'd love to hear what first attracted you to it, George who lives here.

G: I'm really glad you asked that, Jean, because I think that when I answer that question you definitely *will* want to sign up, like me.

J: (*deeply intrigued*) Ooh, perhaps I will! Tell me, George.

G: (*tapping the agreement with his finger*) If you and I sign up – and we have the good fortune to die within a year, guess what we get!

J: What's that then, George?

G: We get a free pen! (*Jean gasps*) Course, our families have to send in the death certificate and all that – to prove we really have died . . .

J: (*they're grown-ups*) Of course. But the pen's a definite?

G: It's here in black and white!

J: A free pen! I'm going to get a form and sign it right now! My family will be over the moon when they find they don't have to pay for my funeral! And your family must be *so thrilled*, George.

G: Oh, they are! My death doesn't seem to bother them at all now they won't have to pay for it! And, of course, if we sign up for the deluxe option, our loved ones will all share a lump sum, too – when we die, that is.

J: (*roguishly*) Not a pen for them, then?

G: (*laughs equally roguishly*) Not on your life! That'll be our little treat, Jean. People like us – the mums and dads, we get the pens, oh yes. Ah, we've had a few laughs here at home lately, I can tell you! Just this weekend my oldest accidentally gave me a little playful push at the top of the stairs when I was about to go down. 'Easy there,' I said, 'or you'll be collecting your lump sum earlier than you thought!'

They laugh loudly, then stop suddenly as if a troubling thought has crossed their minds.

An Odd Mind

I have always had a slightly odd turn of mind. That has not changed. Little questions can result in quite a lot of valuable time being spent working out stuff that seems to be of neither use nor ornament in the normal world. Here is one example. On television very recently one day (possibly it was something like Blue Planet*), the narrator described a type of fish that exists neither in deep waters nor close to shore. The generic term for these creatures was 'pelagic'.*

'Interesting,' I said to myself. 'Clearly this genre of fish needs and deserves a limerick. The years are passing, and I would hate to expire before this worthy task is completed.'

Limericks are not easy. Everything depends on the final line. That line has to make sense, complete the overall thought and rhyme properly with lines one and two. It only took a morning, and, of course, it could not be considered worth the effort by anyone with sense. However, it was done, and I was glad. Let me share my limerick with you.

> *'Because,' said a fish, 'I'm pelagic,*
> *Existence lacks meaning and magic,*
> *Allowed (what a bore),*
> *Neither bottom nor shore,*
> *My life seems insipid and tragic.'*

My wife insisted that, if I was going to talk about the continuing odd workings of my mind as the years go by, I should also mention a brief conversation that occurred recently when we were in the car. Neither of us had spoken for a while. The silence was broken by Bridget asking me a question.

'What are you thinking about?'

Most of us do a swift bit of editing and reordering when that question crops up. I seem to recall someone saying that a clear view of what happens in a person's mind over a period of two minutes might discourage any writer from attempting to put together anything approaching a truly accurate biography. On this occasion I decided, rightly or wrongly, to simply answer Bridget's question.

'Well . . .' I said, after a couple of moments, 'I was thinking about Jung's shadow, the unconscious side of consciousness, then I was asking myself about the illogicality of most thoughts about creation, then I inwardly let out a silent cry of anguish over every damn thing. What else? Yes, then I suddenly thought how much I would love to have a really fresh, dressed crab for supper, and finally I sank into a deep gloom over the difficulty of finding anything near a half-decent radish nowadays. Those are the things I remember.'

It does sound a little strange, I suppose, but perhaps the oddness lies more in my ability to remember every tiny detail more than the actual content of my list? Who knows?

Who Is Saved?

One of the undoubted benefits of growing older is discovering that a lot of things that have seemed terribly serious, and perhaps too challenging to think about with true honesty, simply lose their threat. For me, one of these has been the discussion about who is saved and who is not. I find it interesting that a number of us evangelical Christians seem to drift closer to the pole of universalism (the belief that all will be saved through the resurrection of Jesus) as they advance in years. One or two I have spoken to make it quite clear that they would never express this shift of view in public. It is almost as if they hug the possibility of a broader perspective to themselves.

I really enjoy exploring these questions, usually through the kind of imagined interaction that follows. I've put Q for the questioner and R for the one replying. By the time I had finished writing this piece I think I had arrived at an understanding of where I stand.

But had I? Had I?

Q: I want to ask you something. Why do you go on saying things that put people's backs up? (*pause*) All this stuff about who gets saved, for instance. What's the point?

R: Well, I suppose I feel that someone needs to speak up for God now and then.

Q: Ah, well, there we are, then. That's precisely why they get cross with you, isn't it? They say you're not speaking up for God at all. You're watering down the gospel. Jesus is the only way to salvation. Anyone who doesn't ask him into their lives is lost. Are they wrong?

R: Hmm.

Q: Well, are they?

R: You know, I think it began when I properly registered that verse in Peter's first letter, saying God is not willing that any should be lost. I remember letting those words roll around my head for a time, and then I tried to look really honestly at how they made me feel.

Q: Right. How did they make you feel?

R: Mostly, I felt sorry for God. I really did. The omnipotent, omniscient God wants everyone to be saved, everyone from Genghis Khan to Patience Strong. Don't look so sceptical, surely even Patience Strong must have had a soul. Anyway, that's what he wants, and that is why he became a man who died and came back to life. The logic of that defeats me, as it would any honest person, but the fact remains that he did it to give his dream a chance of being fulfilled. I hate the thought of him being disappointed. Don't you?

Q: Well, yes, of course, but are you saying all humankind will be saved regardless of whether they become Christian believers or not? I mean, that verse in Peter only says God doesn't *want* anyone lost. It doesn't say that he intends to *make* that happen, does it?'

R: No, it doesn't. You're right. Clearly, omnipotence has its limits. No, I suppose I just wanted to help God by flagging up his motivation in all this. We Christians parrot those words about God loving the world so much that he gave his Son, but we may have lost sight, if we ever had it, of the epic passion behind those iconic verses. I just like to remind people that the God they claim to serve is probably greater and more passionately welcoming than any narrow-eyed scrutiny of the spiritual rules and regs might suggest.

The whole idea, believe it or not, is to bring us home, not to study our papers and decide we can't come in because our handwriting has crept over the edge of one small box relating to prejudice against waterfowl.

Q: Stop deliberately trying to make me laugh and answer my question. Before we go any further, you're going to tell me whether Jesus is the only way to home, or heaven, or whatever you call it. It's a simple enough question, surely?

R: Oh, you are such a very cruel person, but I shall submit like the humble person that I am. OK, you win. The older I get the more I am sure, in my heart of heart of heart of hearts, that Jesus is indeed the only means by which we wretched, beloved humans will eventually be able to breathe an eternal sigh of relief. There! That's the good news for those who want to tidy my theology.

Q: (*pause*) Come on, then. The bad news?

R: Ah, well, the bad news – the news that will have them scratching their heads and frowning at a concordance and checking with the elders and praying for my eternal soul – is this. The older I get, the more I am equally sure I have no idea what being saved by Jesus might mean. Let me be honest. Despite being solidly orthodox in my beliefs, I have this blasphemous idea in my head.

Q: I see. And are you going to share your blasphemy with me? Or are you worried that it might be infectious?

R: I do rather hope that it might be exactly that. Tell you what. I'll throw, it's up to you whether you catch or not. My blasphemous thought – and I hardly dare mention it – is that God might do exactly what he wants in exactly the way he chooses. C. S. Lewis talked about surprises in heaven. An understatement, surely. When God casts a net on the right side of his boat, the size and variety of the catch will be astonishing. Many will disagree with me, and they may be right. If I turn out to be in error, I shall discuss the matter with my heavenly Father over a glass of excellent wine in due course. You look a little – troubled.

Q: I suppose it's just that – well, I like the things you say. I want them to be true. But they leave me feeling a bit – unsafe.

32

R: I'm not surprised. It will always feel unsafe to throw open the windows and allow fresh air in when we're busy creating a world where Christianity can only be enjoyed at room temperature. But that kind of caution can have a stifling effect. Besides, as far as this whole question is concerned, it's worth bearing one very important thing in mind.

Q: And that is?

R: It's this. We are the ones who stick on our own spiritual identification labels. Very impressive, some of them are, very ornate and authentic-looking, but, alarmingly – or reassuringly – God is the one who will eventually reach over and, if necessary, simply remove them. Then he will look us in the eye and tell us – exactly – what we actually are. Are you with me?

Q: I'm not sure . . .

Upgrading the Satnav

A small incident that clearly demonstrates the flaws and fascinations of what we prehistoric ones regard as modern technology. We love holidays in France, and Normandy in particular. One of the most anticipated joys is our morning purchase of fresh bread and croissants from the local baker. Our last trip began with a devastating discovery. The local bread supplier had inexplicably decided to take his own two-week holiday during the period when tourists plan their vacations in his village. A pain in the neck. (Geddit?)

We needed to find somewhere a short drive away to supply our needs, so I spoke the French word for 'baker's shop' as clearly as I could into my phone and waited with interest to see what my friend Google might suggest. It was definitely a BOULANGERIE I wanted and asked for, but half a minute later we were supplied with an amazingly long list of places in our part of Normandy where BLUE LINGERIE appeared to be readily available. No contest, of course. Underwear is just cloth – offerings from a French baker constitute a breakfast. However, puzzlement remained. The existence of multiple outlets for blue lingerie in that sparsely populated, particularly rural section of Normandy seemed a surreal, Dali-esque notion.

That strange misdirection aside, we do have a lively appreciation of such technological advances as Google Maps in particular, and satnavs in general.

Here's something that I've been trying to put into words for some time. Cue a rather typically annoying Christian metaphor.

We need to upgrade our spiritual satnavs.

I'm not going to go on about Bridget and me finding our lives changed by the use of a satnav. I've written about that in the past. Suffice it to say that, after years of continually risking divorce through map-reading conflict, we suddenly found ourselves being gently steered through bewildering urban mazes to those churches and halls that seem, for some reason, to be carefully hidden to avoid the danger of being located by itinerant speakers.

Many people say they are not really sure how these devices function. I'm not like them. No – I have not the minutest scrap of a scintilla of a notion how they work. I am just grateful to satellites and NASA scientists and the universe and God and Google that we are now able to get from Upper Dicker to Pratt's Bottom via Godmanchester without killing each other.

Having said all that, there were certainly times in those early satnav days when we discovered that we had come perilously close to abandoning common sense. Our trusted technological guide, in our case 'Katy', would bring us to the bank of a canal or the edge of a cliff and indicate that, ignoring all sane considerations, we should continue in a straight line, just as that gentle voice was directing. The fact is that, ridiculous as it will seem to those who have not experienced this phenomenon, on these occasions both of us experienced a momentary, lunatic urge to launch into the abyss. Why? For heaven's sake, why? Something to do with a misguided respect for technological authority, perhaps? The calm assurance of a familiar voice that is so nearly always right? We never have been sure.

We are now seriously planning to invest in an upgrade to one of the new-age satnavs that are able through Wi-Fi connection to offer travellers immediate notice of changes, problems, obstacles and all sorts of other things connected with events happening in real time on the route that drivers like us are faithfully following. That facility already exists on our phones, of course.

So, here's the thing. Over the last two thousand years, any absence of dynamic and specific direction from God has too often resulted in a whole host of either stolidly traditional or humanly inventive alternatives. I think I understand why that happens. When, for whatever reason, the Holy Spirit doesn't seem to be turning up to prevent us from taking a wrong turn, other schemes and initiatives, many of them quite valuable in themselves, can get shoved in to fill the gap. Here is a selection of some we've come across:

Father, Son and human skills and talents.

Father, Son and an amazing new initiative that's helped thousands of people.

Father, Son and discipleship courses.

Father, Son and a very attractive PowerPoint presentation.

Father, Son and doing what Jesus would have done.

Father, Son and sensible, considered, prayerful decisions.

Father, Son and randomly sprayed-out speeches that sound vaguely prophetic but are actually more like those so-called toilet fresheners that fill the air with something worse than the smells they are supposed to be covering up.

Ironically, another of these is, or can be, 'Father, Son and the Bible as a handbook for life.'

All right. Take it easy. No point calling the Inquisition before you know what I'm going to say. There is, of course, some truth in the idea of the Bible helping to guide us through our lives, but, to return to my fascinating metaphor, there are some Christians who would argue with Jesus himself about Scripture having a greater claim over the course of their lives than he himself does. I have met them. They can be impenetrable. I remember talking to one man who was convinced that the teaching of Jesus indicated clearly that a need he was about to express in prayer would automatically qualify to be supplied in full.

'Could I just ask you something?' I said.

'Yes, of course,' he replied.

'OK – well, suppose Jesus was sitting here in the flesh now, on this chair between you and me.'

'Right.'

'And he said, very nicely, "Look. I understand why this prayer is important to you, but the fact is that I cannot give you what you want at this particular time, nor can I explain the reason for my decision." How would you react?'

He furrowed his brows. A puzzled expression appeared on his face. 'Well,' he said, 'I would definitely have some questions.'

Christianity is and always has been hugely enlivened when it is aware that there is actually a real God, alive and active, working with people and situations, being represented here on Mother Earth by the Holy Spirit, who is quite likely to do something on Wednesday that would have been a complete waste of time last Thursday, and may well never be repeated again.

The idea of upgrading our spiritual satnavs will seriously disturb some people. Just as we thought we'd got God safely contained in systems and traditions and theories and other stuff we've so carefully worked out, in prisons made of words, up he pops, asking us to do the thing that actually needs doing, and to go in the direction that he chooses.

Others will embrace the upgrade, scared and excited at the same time, relieved and liberated by the ingenious leadership of the Holy Spirit, who is alive and well, and is the only one who knows exactly what he's doing.

Of course, it's not as simple as that. Nothing ever is. Nothing ever was. But I wonder how many Christian initiatives, small and magnificently large, have ended up at the bottom of a canal or the foot of a cliff.

Worth a thought, isn't it?

When Things Get Tough

I'm not sure what kind of peace a Christian is supposed to experience. I have been one (a Christian, that is) for fifty-seven years. Sometimes all is well. Sometimes all is definitely not. I know how it feels to be at peace. I certainly know how chaos feels. When I am in the centre of turmoil, I ask Jesus if he knows how I'm feeling. He is very kind.

Do I know the feeling?
Welcome to the cross.
The loss, the fear, the agony, the desolation of desertion,
    and the shame.
Pain and tumult far beyond our understanding.
But hold your nerve, hold the front page, hold these
    words.
I promise you,
In change and shock and wonder,
The peace will be the same.

2

Marching On

I am quite often asked if I think that the Church as a whole has changed for the better since I started writing back in the mid-1980s. Perhaps it has. Generally speaking, it does seem to me that more Christian adherents are tempted to speak the truth these days. That has to be a good thing, of course, but at the same time we have observed that there are certain negative patterns that are repeated again and again.

Recently I reread a book entitled Christian Uncertainties, *written by Monica Furlong, which was published in the 1950s. I was tempted to conclude that it might have been easier and better for me to forget about my own writing and just make sure that this brilliant piece of work was republished every couple of years.*

That would not have worked, of course. I suspect that those negative patterns I mentioned are not going to be eradicated on this side of the Second Coming. They need to be freshly highlighted on a regular basis, because they take individuals and groups into worlds and ways of thinking that are sometimes obvious, occasionally dangerous and often subtle distortions of a truth that can be bewildering enough even in its most simple form.

Every now and then Bridget and I hear about ludicrous incidents, ill-conceived projects or heartbreaking personal histories that will cause one of us, diseased with irony as we are, to exclaim, 'The Church marches on!'

Christian Aid Collection and the Gates of Hell

Everyone after my own heart, and especially those who have saved my life from time to time by smiling quietly wicked smiles in the midst of hellish solemnity, will understand the following assertion.

One of the obstacles that frequently prevents the Church from marching on to victory is a failure to acknowledge the gap between the way things are and the way things are supposed to be.

Examples in my own life? There are too many. Just the thought of them makes my toes curl. Here is one example. Oh, and I promise we will get to the gates of hell eventually – if you see what I mean.

Some years ago I was asked to help with a house-to-house collection of envelopes containing cash contributions for Christian Aid. Earlier in that week the empty envelopes had been popped through the letterboxes of hundreds of homes in the streets surrounding our church in that part of town. My task, a theoretically straightforward one, was to knock or ring the bell at the front doors of houses in three of those streets and simply collect sealed envelopes from those who were happy to give to the cause.

What could possibly go wrong?

Now, the truth is that, even before I started, I didn't want to do it. One man's relatively comfortable gig is another man's descent into the maelstrom. Standing up and speaking to large numbers of people is, generally speaking, not a great problem for me. It happens. It's what I do. However, the prospect of actually inviting sniffy refusals, slammed doors, ill-informed atheistic lectures and chill-infused rejection at an endless succession of private portals filled me with apprehension. Yes, all right, I expect you've done it hundreds of times and are really good at it and have seen many come to faith as a result, but I haven't, and I'm not, and no one came to faith or anything else in my three streets as far as I know. Indeed, some may have found their negative responses to Christianity simultaneously deepened, renewed and refreshed by my visit.

We were furnished with a little unwritten script. After showing our badges (I loathe wearing badges) and explaining that we were there to collect envelopes left by others a few days ago, we were supposed to add, in engaging but unthreatening tones, 'Our church is the one at the top of the hill. We'd love to see you at the ten o'clock service on Sunday mornings if you were ever able to make it.' These words, guaranteed to sound like the worst kind of meaningless drivel when they came out of my mouth, were scheduled to be followed by bright expressions of farewell and a cheery Christian wave as we tripped away down the garden path.

My particular nightmare occurred towards the end of the final street.

I have to confess, incidentally, that overall my task had been marginally less dreadful than I had feared. I developed a very special affection for those who were out when I called. Lovely, thoughtful people. A few elderly folk who were at home greeted me very pleasantly. One or two had actually put money into their envelope and sealed it in readiness for collection. Most people had not done this, and ended up sorting with dull urgency through piles of dog-eared circulars on their hall windowsills while calling out, 'What did you do with that envelope?' to someone buried far away in the bowels of the house. One man, on learning that the collection had a Christian basis, declared aggressively, 'That is not my forte!' The verbal pedant in me simmered and nearly boiled over, but the door was shut in my face before I had a chance to speak.

But my ultimate embarrassment occurred when I was greeted at the front door by a cheerfully amiable woman in her late twenties. Her very substantial top half was seriously unconcealed by a small vest, and she was positively festooned with small children. Leaning sideways and extricating a hand from among the swarm of small squishy bodies, she somehow managed to lift one of the charity envelopes from a cluttered shelf and give it a little shake to indicate that there were coins inside. Seeing how difficult it was for her to bring her hand close to her mouth in order to seal the flap, I spoke five words that were intended to be helpful, but actually sparked a scene that might have come straight out of a film entitled *Carry On Collecting Christian Contributions*.

'I'll lick it for you.'

That's what I said. It triggered an explosion of whooping laughter in my new friend. She turned her head towards the other end of the hall and screamed out, 'Joyce! Come out 'ere a minute! 'E says 'e'll lick it for me!'

A second woman, dressed and festooned in exactly the same style, emerged from the kitchen, whooping happily in chorus as she came, to have a look at me.

'Do you think he'll lick it for me as well?' she asked uproariously.

'I dunno! You'll 'ave to ask 'im!'

Wild hilarity.

I really am not a prude. Those two ladies were just having a bit of fun, and this incident might have passed without too much ongoing trauma, apart from one thing. As I made my retreat along the garden path, clutching the unstuck envelope in one hand, some internal mechanism clicked into action and I heard myself repeating the collector's mantra in a ridiculously shrill voice.

'By the way, our church is the one you can see when you get to the top of the hill. We'd love to see you there at the ten o'clock service on Sunday if you were ever able to make it.'

This precipitated a veritable avalanche of mirth. I hastened from their sight, a real and present danger to porphyrophobics (no, look it up for yourself).

Now, here's an odd thing. As I retreated gratefully in the direction of home, I was suddenly reminded of a verse in Matthew's Gospel that had puzzled and subsequently rather inspired me just before I set off to do my collection that morning. These were the actual words:

And I tell you that you are Peter, and on this rock I will build my church, and the gates of Hades will not overcome it.

(Matt. 16:18)

There are Bible verses we glance over so many times in passing that they almost become invisible. I had never stopped to wonder what these words of Jesus meant. In fact, I had vaguely assumed they were asserting that hell would fail to succeed in attacking and defeating the church. The opposite of what Jesus actually said. What is the matter with me?

In fact, as I realised for the first time that morning, he seemed to be saying that we, the Church, should be battering against the gates of any region where hell has established a stronghold and taken prisoners. My fresh reading of those words indicated that we should be able to knock those gates down with confidence. Go and rescue the lost ones. Get them out and set them free.

Quite often nowadays, Bridget and I see this need when we find ourselves praying with people – a need for us to break in, employing a force that is strange but real, supplied in many different forms and moods by the Holy Spirit, when a lost soul's freedom is the potential prize. It's not just saying a prayer. It's a mindset. An attitude. A watching brief. A readiness to attack. An excitement.

So, I had been considerably fired up by this new thought as I set off in my role as a collector of charity envelopes all those years ago. If I could just get this blasted house-to-house thing finished I would be able to go home and concentrate on those exciting possibilities put forward by Jesus.

Yes, I know it was pathetic. A sort of blindness, I suppose. As I trudged home, I apologised to God for failing to focus on the fact that every single person I had encountered during the morning was crucially important and greatly loved by him. Prisons come in all sorts of shapes and sizes, and they are not always found in a context that is obvious to us.

Nowadays, when I am called to a situation that might require an attack on the gates of hell, I try to shelve personal preference or prejudice. If there is work to be done, I really am up for it – ish.

By the way, those two baby-festooned ladies seemed a country mile away from imprisonment. I do so hope they have enjoyed their lives. And, despite my blushes at the time, I'm sort of glad I gave them a reason to laugh their heads off. Maybe God, who enjoys a laugh himself, will deliberately station them at the gates of heaven ready for my arrival. I would like that.

Risky Living

I suppose my reluctant agreement to go from house to house picking up donations would hardly qualify as risky living in any meaningful spiritual sense. The collection of Christian Aid envelopes definitely did not appear in Paul's horrendous list of the hardships he had endured in the course of his work for God. Actually, contrasting the things we face with that catalogue of horrors does (forgive me, Paul) have its lighter side from time to time.

During the difficult months of Covid lockdown, one of the saving treasures for Bridget and me was our weekly Skype Communion Service with Ken and Liz, our two very good friends. It was a profoundly supportive experience, not least because we were able to relax and laugh a little at ourselves, especially when we arrived, for the umpteenth time, at such challenging liturgical assertions as this:

I offer you my yes to risky living.

We decided to stop and reassess the honesty of our joint claim that we really were positive about the possibility of being thrust into unimaginable suffering if God willed it. On reflection, the unconsidered extravagance with which we made this weekly offering to God amused us no end – but it also made us think. Did we or did we not want to offer our yes to risky living? Yes, we did. Did we mean it? Yes. No. Of course. Maybe. We wanted to.

The thing that really made us laugh – eventually – was the dark coincidence of Ken and Bridget each experiencing quite serious injury within a few days of each other.

Ken stepped back from the bottom of a ladder and trod on a garden rake. The rake flew up and hit him, causing him to fall and hit his head extremely hard on a small, jagged stump sticking up from the ground. Several stitches were needed, and a tooth that had been knocked out had to be replaced.

A few days later, Bridget slipped in a nearby grassy field on the shallowest incline you could imagine, breaking her ankle and dislocating her foot so severely that it was actually facing in the wrong direction. A serious operation followed, and recovery took weeks.

I understand that neither of these incidents sounds very amusing. They were not. On the contrary. However, the thing that did make us laugh when we were finally able to get back to the Communion habit was our reflection that we were unable to avoid trouble and suffering on our own account, let alone through assent to possible problems arising from saying yes to risky living for God.

If, we asked ourselves, we were unable to handle one step back in our own garden or a few steps forward in a field that was as-near-as-dammit flat, how would we get on when the demands of spiritual risky living combined with our accident-prone proclivities?

So, what is the answer to that question? I have no idea. Both? We have no idea. Any attempt to create artificial boundaries in our dealings with God is pointless. Not one of us is forced by God to say yes to risky living. But perhaps if we gather together determination and gratitude and all the trust we can muster and offer the most honest 'yes' we can manage, it will be taken seriously. We will be agreeing to do whatever is needed to make his plans work. Risky? Of course.

They're Not a Bad Bunch

I think Bridget and I have finally faced the fact that we are as strange and difficult in our own way as anybody else. This is particularly relevant in the Church, where differences abound and each person has a view. Having said that, every now and then two people almost agree.

They're not a bad bunch in our church,
I love lots of things that we do.
But one thing prevents us from reaching consensus:
Everyone has their own view.

I think we agree there's a God,
Though Jack's not quite sure, to be fair.
Anne said to Jack he was heading for hell,
Jack said, 'I am if you're there.'

Mary thinks tongues is an obsolete gift,
But June said, 'I'm using it now!'
Mary told June she was wrong in the head;
On Sunday they had a huge row.

They said dreadful things to each other,
And push very soon came to shove.
The noise got so bad that the pastor went mad,
But they said, 'No, we're fighting in love.'

He replied, 'You are not! So stop talking rot,
I could hear you from two floors above!'
They said, 'What a fuss! You're louder than us.'
He said, 'Yes, but I'm shouting in – oh, for goodness'
    sake!'

Actually – some are not keen on our pastor,
But Mary and Joan think he's hot.
I reckon young Lee would like to agree,
But he's not left his closet – not yet.

Caroline aches in her joints when his points
Don't start with identical letters.
Vaughn says his talks are like long winter walks,
And June hates the length of his sweaters.

Look – it's not that we don't like opinions –
It's healthy to share what we think –
But when some have their say it's like flowers in May,
With others it's more of a stink.

But they're not a bad bunch in our church,
I love loads of things that we do.
Just one thing prevents us from reaching consensus:
Everyone has their own view.

Says you.
And you – well, most of the time.
Huh! Talk about the cat calling the block petal.
What did you say?
You heard.
I did not!
I meant, talk about the pet calling the clock – oh, never
    mind . . .

Individual Differences

Here's a question. Does the great army of God march in step? I suspect the honest answer is that it does, and should – apart from those who don't, and shouldn't.

Do you remember the television programme called *The Secret Millionaire*? I think most countries have their own version nowadays. In each episode a multimillionaire goes under cover for a couple of weeks in a deprived area, with a view to giving away thousands of pounds of his or her own money to deserving causes at the end of the stay. Of course, the presence of a camera crew has to be explained away, but that never seems to be much of a problem.

Leaving aside the uncomfortable awareness that my emotions are no doubt being expertly manipulated by the programme makers, I always find it a very moving thing to watch. The featured projects and enterprises are invariably run by genuine, humble people who are working hard to make a difference in very difficult circumstances, and their astonishment on being presented with such huge and unexpected financial windfalls appears unfeigned.

A few words spoken at the end of one programme in the series struck me very forcibly. They came from one of two men who run a boxing club in Northern Ireland for lads who might otherwise be getting into all sorts of trouble on the streets of Belfast. On being handed a cheque that would make it possible to find new and more appropriate premises for the club, this fellow looked into the camera lens with an expression of shocked bewilderment on his face, and said the following words: 'You think you're alone – but you're not!'

I've been thinking about that ever since, and particularly about the fact that this man's experience is precisely what so many Christians (and non-Christians) long for. Not the money exactly, but the stunning immediacy of God sweeping benevolently into their lives to prove that they are not alone, that he does care, and that he really can make a significant difference to the situation they find themselves in.

Experience suggests that if I were to say this publicly I would be pretty swiftly buttonholed and reminded or informed that this is exactly what God does do when men and women ask Jesus into their lives. So what on earth am I talking about? Well, whatever anyone says, it really is not as simple as that, is it? Let us suppose that someone were to ask you or me the following very simple question: 'What should I expect to happen when I become a Christian?

What will God actually do? How will I feel? What will change?'

When I think of the Christians I've known and the stories they have been good and generous enough to share with me, I have to accept that there are all sorts of answers to that query.

A few possibilities.

Nothing. That's what happens to quite a lot of people. Jesus suggests in the Parable of the Prodigal Son that the Father will throw his arms around sons and daughters who return home, shower them with gifts and throw a party to celebrate their homecoming. And yet, many people who would call themselves Christians have never experienced this explosive encounter. They have experienced nothing. Nothing at all. Leaving aside the non-trivial fact that, on the most important level of all, they have been granted eternal life and total forgiveness, there is no actual evidence to suggest that God is any more or less present than he was before the prayer was prayed or the commitment made. Generations of nervous preachers and evangelists have somehow managed to turn this deficiency into a virtue.

'You don't have to worry,' they burble optimistically. It's a good thing, really. 'You see, quite a lot of people don't actually experience anything at the time. It's a matter of faith, you see. Trust God and the future will bring all sorts of blessings. Take a step into the darkness. There'll be light on the other side. You'll see!'

Sometimes this prediction is absolutely spot on. The future does bring real, perceptible blessings. Sometimes it doesn't. Why is that? Answers on a postcard please.

For other new converts, the answer is that *every* blessed

thing happens. They speak in tongues. They prophesy. They enjoy a powerful sense of God being with them, filling body and soul with a knowledge of his love and care. They fall off their horses on the road to Damascus, hear Jesus talking to them, go blind, get healed and end up taking the gospel to the Gentiles.

I have a friend, once a frighteningly dangerous, violent man, who knelt down in the cell of his high-security prison and asked God to change his life. At that moment and with permanent effect his life was transfigured. He was a new man. A wonderful, old-fashioned, tin-tabernacle miracle. Fantastic for those who begin their Christian lives with such dramatic encounters. Puzzling and a little intimidating for those who don't.

Some people would deny that they ever crossed an identifiable spiritual starting line. Perhaps they grew up in a Christian family where being a follower of Jesus seemed as natural and inevitable as breathing, and in most cases their faith seems no less genuine for that.

At least two people I know became Christians primarily through fear. I hope and pray that they have subsequently learned something about the love that has fought so bravely to dispel our dread of being lost in the universe, but there is no doubt that the threat of hell prodded these folk towards repentance in the first place. No problem with that really, I suppose. Jesus was very strong on the subject.

Perhaps the reason so few people switch on to the good news is that they have never been helped to comprehend the bad news. I know that the concept of hell is not too fashionable in some quarters of the church nowadays, but I would respectfully suggest that those who embrace this view should check that God has managed to keep up with contemporary theological thinking. He can be a bit slow and obtuse sometimes.

I've only mentioned four possibilities for those who want to know how God will greet them when they first turn to him. There are many, many others. Why the differences? Why doesn't God issue an identical emotional and spiritual starter pack to every convert, just to reassure them that they're on the right track?

Sidestepping the responsibility of answering such a difficult question, I can only offer a couple of reflections.

First of all, I would suggest that some conversions are not conversions at all. One of my favourite writers is Paul Tournier, a Swiss doctor who spent years counselling Christians in trouble. Stepping into the world of his relaxed, compassionate wisdom is like dropping into a gently bubbling hot tub at the end of a wearying day. He quietly explained to one of his patients that it was almost certainly the nature of his so-called conversion that was choking general growth and the specific development of peace in his life.

Some Christians may find this sort of thing very difficult to accept, of course. Conversion is a significant feature in the 'Being a Christian' kit, and it seems like a sort of heresy even to question the validity of such a sacred event. However, as we all know, life simply is not like that.

It is worth noting that the Sailors' Society began in the nineteenth century after one of its founders spotted a notice outside a church that read 'No Sailors or Prostitutes'. We, as a worldwide Church, are still dealing with a legacy of intolerance and Phariseeism from sniffily respectable religious organisations. Even worse, we are allowing new varieties to develop. These may appear very different. Some, confident they have escaped this problem, have developed an equally excluding tolerance.

Conversion can be a good example. Those who do not experience appropriate change might find that their lack of visible progress is rebuked and disciplined. How dare they spoil the game for others? They feel guilty and unhappy. Common sense tells them one thing; their church tells them another. How can this be? Sadly, it is possible for churches to master the art of performing and expounding something that looks so like Spirit-filled Christianity that it is almost impossible to tell the genuine from the false.

So, sticking the 'conversion' label on to an experience doesn't in itself necessarily mean anything. You can unstick it. You might need to. God will help you. You might feel a damn sight better afterwards. We really do need to hang on to the truth of our own experiences. We are allowed to be different. It's all right. God is in charge of change.

A few months ago I made the mistake of tuning in to one of those blow-wave evangelists who stride up and down platforms in wildly expensive suits, trumpeting the most mundane spiritual truths as though they hadn't existed in the Bible until they discovered them last Tuesday, leaving long dramatic pauses that don't mean or do anything at all other than invite applause, and persuading docile congregations to repeat dismal little half-arsed mantras like parrots to each other and – oh, Lord, save us!

Anyway, this particular character said something that made me want to burst through the television screen and strangle him with his own Italian silk tie – just to show him that I understood more about the love of God than he did, if you get my drift. These were his words, delivered in the solemn, soupily pedagogic, Thatcherite tones of one who is telling us something we need to know for our own good, even though we might not like it: 'The only thing in you that God loves is Jesus . . .'

What a horrible thing to say. What a sad and inexplicable denial of all that life and the Bible teaches about God's very individual, caring relationships with his people. The prodigal son. Peter. John. Cornelius. David. Jonah. Jacob. Elijah. Me. You. Brenda. Malcolm. The list would have to go on until we have included every single person who, in the entire history of the world, ever interacted with the living, loving, bewildering, vulnerable God.

So if I discover it really is true that the only thing that God loves in me is Jesus, I might take out a subscription to my local Ember Day Bryanite assembly and seek fulfilment there. As I have frequently said, each of us is different, and those differences, loved and respected by a God who knows from experience exactly how it feels to be a human being, are bound to affect the way in which we approach and perceive the invitation that he extends. Thus, for people who have been badly hurt and betrayed in relationships by those who should have been looking after them, it may take years or even a lifetime for the process of being born again to be completed. As we all know, every church has its little contingent of these folk who patently never quite manage the 'spiritual stuff' that's supposed to happen. They are not warts on the Body of Christ. They are not bad adverts for what we believe. They *are* the Body of Christ.

The quick-fix merchants can say what they like about this. Miraculous change does sometimes occur, but the fact remains that many Christians are so broken up inside by negative circumstances and cruelty suffered in the past that they can only survive through years of love, attention and practical concern from believers who are fortunate enough to have a little stability and charity to spare and share. And let's be honest, these sparers and sharers may have to go on doing their thing until the moment when the two of them walk arm in arm through the gates of heaven as equals, and Jesus smilingly congratulates them both on making it.

Individual differences. They can make all the difference.

I could go on and on, but it might become boring. And in the final analysis, of course, I have to confess that I am not privy to God's motivation in either allowing or causing such wildly varying experiences of himself to those who reach out to receive his love. Who knows what is going on behind the scenes? Who knows what battles have to be fought, what devilish manoeuvres have to be thwarted, how much darkness has to be dispelled so that Emily Dunworthy of 16 Dibley Road, Penge, can reach a point where she thinks she might have a sort of feeling that she has possibly experienced a tentative sense of the reality of God?

I suspect that the Holy Spirit is a divine opportunist when it comes to drawing in the objects of his passion, and perhaps that is the most important consideration in the end. However we come to faith, no matter how disappointingly uneventful or excitingly dramatic the experience may have been, we are facing in the same direction, we are hopefully in good company, and the best is yet to come.

I am as confused by the whole business as I ever was, but a glow of excitement inside prompts me to say to non-believers and troubled believers alike the words that burst from that surprised chap on *The Secret Millionaire*: 'You think you're alone – but you're not.'

The Attitudes

The Beatitudes (Matt. 5:3–10) are special fruit, are they not? A spectacular benefit to those who hunger and thirst after extra layers of truth about the way things are in the kingdom of God. Perplexing and paradoxical, they rarely fail to offer something new. What would happen, I wondered, if one were to consider their diametrical opposites? An interesting thought.

Blessed are the poor in spirit,
for theirs is the kingdom of heaven.

Blessed are the publicly strong and mighty in spirit,
for they shall be able to enjoy making other believers feel
    like failures
and doubt that they were ever really Christians at all.

Blessed are those who mourn,
for they will be comforted.

Blessed are those who have no sympathy, empathy or
    anything else ending with the same three letters;
after all, sadness is surely a sign of weakness,
for they won't need comforting,
seeing as they couldn't care less about anybody else.

Blessed are the meek
for they will inherit the earth.

Blessed are those who are up themselves,
for they shall be listened to and have their ideas acted on,
even when the things the meek suggested made much
    more sense,
but no one heard what they said because the up-them-
    selves-ones were so loud and mouthy.

**Blessed are those who hunger and thirst for righteousness,
for they will be filled.**

Blessed are those who hunger and thirst for
    unrighteousness,
for they shall be free to do all sorts of horrible things,
and if the whole God/heaven thing turns out to be a load
    of rubbish,
it won't really matter, will it?

**Blessed are the merciful,
for they will be shown mercy.**

Blessed are those who think forgiveness is soft and weak,
for they shall be correct until the very moment when they
    wish they were not.

**Blessed are the pure in heart,
for they will see God.**

Blessed are those who nurse and feed on the nasty, dismal
    things inside them,
for they are very unlikely to want to see God anyway.

Blessed are the peacemakers,
for they will be called children of God

Blessed are those who cause war and misery all over the
 world,
and thrice blessed are those who create conflict in places
 where there wasn't any until they turned up,
for they shall be able to have a laugh at everyone else's
 expense,
and never be embarrassed by being called children of
 God.

Blessed are those who are persecuted because of
 righteousness,
for theirs is the kingdom of heaven.

Blessed are those who change sides when things get too
 hot for comfort,
for there are limits, you know, even in the kingdom of
 heaven – surely?

Walthamstow Bible Study

Some of the sketches that Bridget and I perform are received
with an incredulity that can be either positive or negative.
The 'Walthamstow Bible Study' is a good example of this.
Those who have endured church meetings in which their
search for depth has been thwarted by focused questioning
and superficial responses might find it very heartening. At
last, somebody seems to actually recognise that this sort of
thing happens.

Others, on the other hand, find it difficult to accept that, for apparently inexplicable reasons, familiar ways of approaching the Bible, and those who meet to discuss scriptural passages in this way, are being lampooned and treated with scant respect.

I love them all.

JUNE: (*completing her reading of Bible passage*) '. . . but stayed out in the country; and people came to him from every quarter'[2].

LEADER: Right! Thank you so much, June. OK, we've read the passage. Now, I've got the minister's questions here. Question one – and it's a good one. Do we think the leper was pleased or upset to be healed? Do we think the leper was *pleased* or *upset* to be healed? Food for thought. Why don't we all drop into the shampoo position for just a moment and ask the Lord to help us find the answer to that question. (*pause while all study*) So, what do we all think? Was the leper pleased or upset to be healed? Anyone? Yes, Julie?

JULIE: (*tentatively*) Erm, I think he was pleased.

LEADER: (*nodding seriously*) Thank you, Julie, interesting. You think he was pleased. And he was pleased because . . . (*encourages all with gestures*) Yes, Jackie?

JACKIE: Could it have been – because he was healed?

LEADER: Good! He was pleased because he was healed. The leper was healed, and so he was pleased. A lot to think about there. Anybody else? Mm! Janine?

JANINE: Can I just say, I think he was very pleased.

---

[2] Mark 1:45

LEADER: Wow! The leper was *very* pleased because he was healed. He was healed, and he wasn't just pleased, he was very pleased. That's very special. Thank you, Janine.

FOLKS, I think we've probably got about as far as we can go with that for now. So, June, Julie, Jackie and Janine, let's thank God for the abundant fruit of his Word by moving into a time of praise and worship. June, would you like to lead us please?

JUNE: Yes, of course. I thought we could begin by singing number 3492 in *Remission Hymnal*. 'What's the use of rushing around in, for instance, Walthamstow, when you haven't got God in your life?' And we'll sing it – twenty-nine times?

ALL SING: What's the use of rushing around in, for instance, Walthamstow,

What's the use of rushing around in, for instance, Walthamstow,

What's the use of rushing around in, for instance, Walthamstow,

If you haven't got God in your life?

LEADER: I don't think we'll bother with the other twenty-eight . . .

Sitting in Rows Waiting for Something to Happen

There are little villages, particularly in Yorkshire, that Bridget and I quite often pass through or near to on our busy way to somewhere else. We tell each other that we shall explore them all one by one and discover what they have to offer. We have done exactly that on a few occasions

and rarely been disappointed. Yorkshire is filled with honey-coated secrets.

The same process occurs with bits of the Bible that I have noticed but never fully explored. Here is an example.

Jesus tells this very short story about a father and his two sons in the twenty-first chapter of Matthew's Gospel.

> 'What do you think? There was a man who had two sons. He went to the first and said, "Son, go and work today in the vineyard."
>
> ' "I will not," he answered, but later he changed his mind and went.
>
> 'Then the father went to the other and said the same thing. He answered, "I will, sir," but he did not go.
>
> 'Which of the two did what his father wanted?'
>
> 'The first,' they answered.
>
> Jesus said to them, 'Truly I tell you, the tax collectors and the prostitutes are entering the kingdom of God ahead of you. For John came to you to show you the way of righteousness, and you did not believe him, but the tax collectors and the prostitutes did. And even after you saw this, you did not repent and believe him.'
>
> (Matt. 21:28–32)

When I did stop to think about these words, the central meaning of the parable seemed clear. The man represents God, and the sons symbolise two classes of Jews: the Pharisees with their followers, and the lawless and sinful who never made any pretence of religion. The former, who profess to keep the Law strictly, reject Jesus. The latter, who have no religious status at all, respond to Jesus and become believers.

So far so good, and so not surprising. But as I read the passage again, something nagged at my memory. It took me a while, but I got there at last.

It was a long time ago. I had been asked to speak at a men's day organised by a church in the west of England. My brief was to prepare two half-hour talks that would punctuate longer morning and afternoon addresses by the keynote speaker, a well-known evangelist from somewhere in Scotland. Perfectly reasonably, those who were planning the day wanted to ensure that my contribution would be relevant and helpful to men in particular. I happen to be a man, so that helped.

I put quite a lot of thought into preparing my two talks. The lists of headings were neatly typed in capital letters on two sheets of paper and clipped into a new blue folder that Bridget had bought for me the day before. My spontaneous asides fluttered around my head like tame butterflies. My second-best glasses were tucked into the top pocket of my shirt. I was ready to go.

I had done a few of these events over the years, and as I entered the venue and took my seat on the front row, I was impressed by the numbers in the hall. There must have been more than two hundred men there, sitting in rows, waiting for whatever was on offer.

The event began with what is popularly referred to as a time of worship. I can become truly lost and significantly found in a period of sensitive worship, but what followed was not sensitive. It was emotionally brutal and short-sighted. I hated it.

After a brief welcome from one of the organisers, five men on guitars, keyboard, violin and drums exploded into action with shocking abruptness. The lead singer, an apparently weightless, slightly feral young man afflicted with some kind of stillness allergy and very strange hair, made the musicians behind him look positively comatose. He was wild, and it was weird.

Halfway through the first instalment of musical frenzy, the two hundred men were loudly instructed to rise from their seats so that they could celebrate the presence of the Lord who saves and heals and overcomes and goodness knows what else. Turning my head to look out over the hall, I witnessed a sight that has always troubled me. Some of the men, mainly the ones who were sitting nearest to the front, seemed to have successfully entered the ecstasy. A much larger proportion of the audience or congregation had not entered anything, other than a slow-motion paroxysm of embarrassment and unease.

I would have found it difficult to put my feelings into words in those days. Nowadays I can. Many of those fellows must have come to this event in the tender hope that confusion and doubt and inadequacy and fear of failure might be seriously addressed and eased. Now they had been precipitated into what must have seemed a hellish expectation that everything had to begin with a blatant, corporate act of dishonesty. They were doing their best to comply. There was a lot of uneasy bobbing, a few rictus grins and a desperate shifting of the eyes as it became clear that flight was not an option.

This might not have been quite so bad if the session had lasted for ten minutes or so, but it did not. It went on for three-quarters of an hour. Surely, I said to myself as I sat glumly waiting for the Second Coming, there is enough misery in the world without adding forty-five minutes of frenetic so-called worship.

It was not fair. And, as I discovered later during the lunch interval, it was counterproductive. The uncompromising emotional and religious demands of that first forty-five minutes had caused some of the chaps who spoke to me to retreat rather than advance. For all sorts of different reasons, they were not yet people who could honestly leap and bounce, rejoicing in a God who, as far as they knew, might or might not come to their rescue. Sadly, they had been alienated, not drawn in.

So, what's the connection with that Parable of the Two Sons? I suppose, in a modern context, the son who announced so enthusiastically that he would go and do as he was told might have demonstrated his apparent respect and love for his father by singing and dancing and loudly expressing his absolute determination to carry out the task in question. Possibly it would have sounded extremely impressive.

Father, dear father,
My love is strong and true,
To do your will is all I ask –
I'll tend the vines for you.
I gladly offer all of me,
Every little bit,
Unlike my younger brother,
Who's a grumpy little git.

All that would have meant nothing. He didn't do it.

The other son, speaking out of the place where he found himself in relation to his father, would have said the same thing whatever the context. He wasn't going to go, and possibly it was a very graceless refusal. Who knows what was actually going on inside him? Later, something happened. There was a genuine change of heart. He found a reason to become a son who was willing to obey his father. Good news.

There are no easy lines to draw here. Sung worship can be wonderful and effective, but as dear old Tozer is reputed to have said, 'Christians don't tell lies, they go to church and sing them.' An overstatement perhaps, but if we make the mistake of assuming that noise and energy are worthy substitutes for obedience and sensitive engagement with individuals, we may miss an essential side turning and, even though spring is bursting out all over, have a very unseasonal awakening.

Shoes

The knowledge that freedom is born in reality has hopefully always been an important part of the work done by the Church. Easy to say, but the judgement as to what is real and what is not can create many problems.

There can be a very fine line between over-spiritualising and failing to allow the Spirit freedom in our lives and the lives of others. The following sketch features a telephone call between a lady with an overwhelming appetite for ministry and a member of the church community who is actually struggling with a very practical issue. The original version was written many years ago and reminds me of a time in my life when I was dealing with precisely the same problem as Ted.

RACHEL: Ah! Hello! Ted?

TED: Ted here, yes. Who's that?

R: Rachel here, Ted. Rachel Bellbrook. Hi.

T: Oh yes, hello, Rachel. What can I do for you? I'm a bit—

R: Ted, can I speak to you as a friend – a spiritual sister?

T: I don't know, Rachel. Have a go and see.

R: Ha, ha, very good, Ted. Very good. Seriously though, I just rang on the off-chance of having a friendly chat and seeing how you are. To see how you're getting along. Catch up on the old news. Find out how the cookie's crumbling at your end of the packet. No special reason for calling. Just a friendly, er, call.

T: Oh, right. Fine.

Pause.

R: So, er, how are you?

T: Fine, Rachel. I'm fine, thanks.

R: Good, good. Wife OK?

T: Fine.

R: Kids?

T: They're fine.

R: Work?

T: Work's fine.

R: Car going all right?

T: Bike. Had to sell the car when—

R: Bike going OK?

T: Oh, pedalling along nicely, thanks.

R: Any golf recently? A little bird tells me you haven't been up to the club for a while.

T: Can't afford it, Rachel, not since I lost—

R: Surviving without it, eh?

T: Oh, yes, fine!

R: Good, good. Surviving without the golf. So, generally speaking you're . . .

T: Fine, Rachel. Generally speaking, I'm just fine.

R: Good! Great! Wonderful! Marvellous! (*pause*) Fine.

Pause.

T: Was that all, Rachel, because I really ought to—

R: Saw you in church on Sunday, Ted.

T: Good. And I saw you, Rachel.

R: Did you?! Yes! Good! So, we were, er, both there, then.

T: Looks that way, Rachel. Yep.

R: (*casually*) Didn't see you up at the old Communion rail, though, Ted. (*pause*) No sign of you kneeling up at the, er, Communion rail to, er, take Communion. (*pause*) No, er . . . bread or wine for you this Sunday, then?

T: That's right, Rachel.

R: Nor the Sunday before that, I seem to recall.

T: Nope!

R: Nor the Sunday before that, Ted.

T: Nor the Sunday before that, if you must know, Rachel.

R: Ted, if you're having trouble at home, I'm sure it can be sorted out. I'm more than happy to come and talk it through with you. Getting angry with your wife? Evil thoughts? Not pulling your weight in the home? Adultery? Shouting at the kids? Some little private sin? Are you gay, Ted?

T: Rachel, it's not—

R: There is no reason why you shouldn't kneel at the Communion rail like anyone else, Ted. If you've got the time, I've got the ministry, and though I say it myself, I do have a bit of a special gift when it comes to leading lost brothers and sisters through confession to repentance. Speak up, Ted. You can't shock me. What is it? Covetousness? Theft? Been dabbling in the occult?

T: For goodness' sake!

R: Drink? Drugs? Unbelief? Come on, Ted! What is it that's preventing you from kneeling at that rail? Cheating on tax? Spirit of criticism? What's keeping you in your seat on Sunday mornings? Greed? Spiritual pride? Idolatry?

T: Don't be ridiculous. It's just—

R: Ted, are we in the same Christian family?

T: Yes, different planet, but—

R: Do we trust each other?

T: Yes, but—

R: Is there anything you'd keep from me, Ted?

T: No, but it's—

R: So what's the problem, bro? Open up and—

T: (*through gritted teeth*) Don't ever call me bro!

R: Look, open up and share the problem, Ted. I've watched you every Sunday looking troubled when it's time for Communion, and I know – I just know, my dear brother, that something is preventing you from walking down the centre aisle and kneeling to receive a blessing. I feel led to counsel you now that the time has come to reveal any secret sin and find freedom.

T: I haven't got a secret sin. Chance would be a fine thing! It's just—

R: (*loudly*) Now is the time for courage. Gird your loins and—

T: I'll do what I like with my loins.

R: Make that decision to unburden yourself. Ted, he will not strive forever, and this is the acceptable day. Why can't you kneel at the Communion rail?

T: Look, it's actually none of your—
R: Tell me why you cannot kneel at that Communion rail, Ted.
T: Because I've got holes in my shoes!

Heart to Head

A pet mantra in the Christian youth group I attended as a teenager was about the fact that some people had acquired faith (or Jesus) in their heads, but this awareness or acquisition had not travelled the eighteen inches down to their hearts.

One day I might strangle a mantra.

In the meantime, it is worth saying that, for people like you, perhaps, and certainly for me at one point in my life, the opposite may be true. We have something that burns or smoulders or flickers stubbornly in our hearts, but over time has become rather lifelessly lodged in our heads. That gradual but profound change may not be easy to handle for all sorts of reasons, but that heart truth is something important to hug to ourselves when darkness comes down and words grow slack, as good old T. S. Eliot might have said. The liturgy of the heart does not need and cannot use many words, but it is no less genuine, and possibly even more authentic, than some common verbal expressions of faith.

We need to value the private place in us where only God sees and hears and knows what we need before we ask.

We must not give in.

We need to hold our nerve.

We shall be needed.

3

Adrian Plass and the Summer Festival

I suppose it was inevitable that the fictional characters from that first Sacred Diary of Adrian Plass *would become like members of our own family as the years went by. More* Sacred Diaries *followed as time passed, and as we travelled around this country and other parts of the world we did our best to answer the same questions many times.*

Is there really a Gerald?

Why is your wife called Bridget when her name is Anne in the book?

Why did Leonard Thynn borrow the cat?

Are you as funny in real life as you are when you're trying to write funny stuff?

Aren't you worried that non-Christians reading your Diary books might think the Church really is like that?

Recently, some of the old characters came alive again when I was asked to write an account of Adrian's experiences at a new Christian festival. As usual, it became an opportunity to look at what really goes on in such worlds, by contrast with what is supposed to happen.

A little exaggerated? Well, perhaps, but here is the answer I have so often given when asked where I find humour in the Church: 'You only have to be awake and be there.'

I may be wrong, of course.

Friday, 10 a.m.
Off today with Anne my wife, Gerald my son, who used to be flippant and unemployed but is now flippant and an Anglican priest, and our wonderful daughter-in-law Josey, fully recovered from a recent serious illness. Can't wait to get to the new combined summer Christian festival. They've come up with a very neat title in my view:

BIG DAYS OUT FOR THE GREEN UPRISING SURVIVORS OF NEW WINE IN GLORY

So good to have something entirely original.

Friday, 9 p.m.
Arrived quite late this evening (first big celebration is tomorrow evening). So glad we opted for a chalet instead of camping. Used to enjoy it, but hopefully the next very small space to receive my chilled body in the dark will be my coffin. All very excited, but dog-tired. I shall keep up diary entries until I run out of steam . . .

Friday, 11 p.m.
Heart-sinking news. From my point of view anyway. Anne left telling me until late tonight, knowing it would depress me. Minnie Stamp from our church rang Anne earlier to ask if she could come down tomorrow evening and Anne said she could take the unoccupied third room in our chalet for a couple of days.

Minnie is my nemesis, the person from our church who makes my blood boil more than just about anybody else in the world. I've written about her in my diary before. She's the one who reacts to anything I say as if I've asked for counselling, and the way she says my name with her little speech impediment on the 'r' drives me bonkers, even though it shouldn't.

Sometimes I think if it wasn't for people like Minnie, Christianity would be a piece of cake.

Can't believe I just wrote that.

Saturday, 8 a.m.
Said to Anne after we got into bed last night, 'You know, I might have been a bit unfair to Minnie. I think I'll tell her tomorrow how I honestly feel about her and apologise for my bad thoughts. What do you think?'

Anne said, 'Adrian, I've never forgotten her saying that you were the fairy light on God's Christmas tree, and that everyone loves your twinkle. I reckon the less you say, the less there is for her to misinterpret. It's up to you, though, sweetheart.'

Turned my plan over in my mind before going to sleep. Anne's very wise, but you know what – that doesn't mean she's always right.

Lots of seminars to choose from.
Decided to leave today's seminar selection to the Holy Spirit. Cut out strips from a copy of the programme naming every available meeting. Folded each one up small and put the ten o'clock ones in a balaclava I'd brought from home by accident, the eleven-thirty ones in an empty teabag box, the two o'clock ones in a heavy metal vase from the chalet sitting room and the three-thirty ones in one of Anne's slippers. Placed all four things in a row, sat with my hand hovering over the balaclava and closed my eyes to pray.

Anne came in. Looked a little worried and said, 'Darling, what are you doing?'

Opened my eyes and explained that, after ending up at too many seminars full of flow charts and Venn diagrams and brainstorming over the last couple of years, I'd decided to give the whole thing to God and let him direct me to the place where he wishes me to go.

Anne said, 'Well, I hope he has better luck than me. You're never very keen to be directed to anywhere I wish you would go. Seriously, Adrian, don't you think God might prefer you to use your common sense and just choose a few things that take your fancy?'

Closed my eyes again and picked one piece of paper out of the balaclava. Tucked it in my top pocket without looking to see what it was.

I said, 'Anne, my hope and prayer is that this and the other three seminars that I am about to pick out will provide my spiritual food for the day. I shall attend the first one at ten o'clock this morning. Let's have some breakfast.'

Not looking forward to seeing Minnie Stamp this evening. Still, I feel quite confident that my new approach will clear the air.

Saturday, lunchtime
New way of beginning the first full day of the festival. Everyone gets a note saying they have to go to an SEG (Spiritual Encounter Group) for twenty minutes before the sessions start. Gerald and I found ourselves in the same group, thank goodness. Fifteen people sitting in a circle, all wearing our new name badges. Looked round, wondered if

we might have been allocated to the wrong group. Slightly strange collection of us. A bit – specialised?

A little surprised when the leader (very earnest, and aged thirty-two going on fourteen according to Gerald) told us we had to turn to the person next to us and describe something shameful that we'd done. For goodness' sake!

I had a very small, thin, nervous-looking man called Brian on my right, and a huge man called Norman with a ferocious glare and very long arms on my left. Brian took quite a long time leading up to confessing that he had accepted the gift of an unexpired parking ticket from someone in a car park. He had defrauded the local council of fifty pence. Did I think he would be forgiven, and could I help him pray through to peace?

Did that.

Turned to the enormous man. He said, 'I murdered Jean Shrimpton.'

Bit shocked for a moment.

I said, 'I'm sorry – do you mean Jean Shrimpton, the famous 1960s model?'

He nodded, staring into my eyes and making horrible strangling movements with his hands. I pointed out that, to my certain knowledge, Jean Shrimpton was still alive. He said, 'Oh, I think I meant a different Jean Shrimpton. Yes, I did mean a different Jean Shrimpton, one who *is* dead because I murdered her. Or – now I think about it, it might not have been her. It might have been Arnold Schwarzenegger.'

I said sternly but gently, 'Now, Norman, I don't think we've murdered anybody at all, have we?'

He wrapped his arms around me (twice, Gerald said later) and told me I had changed his life for ever.

Doubt that somehow.

I confessed some minor tax avoidance to Brian, and an unevenly adjusted faith–family balance to Norman. Both visibly unimpressed and disappointed by my shameful things.

After that the leader said we all had to tell the group ten things that God had done for us that day. Bit early in the morning for that, I thought. God hadn't really got going with me yet. Also, I was last to speak, so all the best ones had got used up by other people. Did my best.

I said brightly, 'God has given me ten new brothers and sisters to love, right here in this circle that we're sitting in.'

Thought this was rather good, but they got tense and agitated and wanted to know why four people in the group were not new brothers and sisters given to me by God to love, and would I tell them which ones they were?

Got a bit flustered and said, 'Well, one of them is my son.'

Short silence, then someone said worriedly, 'Has God not given you your son to love, then?'

I said, 'What? Of course, but he's not new, is he? And the other three *are* new brothers and sisters to love, but I was asked to say ten things, so that's what I did. Look! I love you all, right? All my new brothers and sisters. I love all – how many is it? – all thirteen of you.'

Realised that I was actually beginning to quite dislike the new brothers and sisters I'd been given to love. Quite relieved when it ended and we could go. Asked Gerald what shameful thing he'd confessed to.

He said, 'Oh, my stock answer. I said I'd been dabbling in the medieval heresy of Modalism.'

'Did they like that?'

'Loved it! Absolutely loved it. One of the new brothers and sisters we've been given to love cast it out of me.'

'Is it gone?'

'Hard to say. She said it was, but I can only vaguely remember what it is, so it might still be there.'

Thought for a while as we walked across the field, then said, 'Gerald, do you think there's something a bit odd about us?'

He said, 'Interesting question, Dad. Yes. I think we are – oddly normal.'

Arrived at the place called the 'Speaking Hub' ten minutes early. Quite excited to see which seminar I would be directed to first by the Holy Spirit. Unfolded the paper from my top pocket and read what it said.

ADMINISTRATIVE PARAMETERS IN THE CONTEXT OF DISENCODED SEMANTICS

Didn't look too promising on the face of it but decided to trust and believe that I would receive spiritual food through the seminar leader. Took a notebook and biro into the venue, sat on the front row, opened my notebook, clicked my biro and waited for God to speak.

Ran into my son three years later just outside the venue. Showed him the title.

He said, 'Hmm, not exactly the Second Coming, is it? Can I see what you put in your notebook?'

'No.'

'Oh, go on.'

'If you insist.'

I showed him. 'OK – this, Gerald, is a little house with windows and a front door and smoke coming out of the chimney. I used to do it for you when you were little because it was the only thing I could draw. Next is the first line of the Lord's Prayer written backwards with my left hand to see if I could do it. Ah, yes, these are three games of noughts and crosses I played against myself. Somehow managed to lose two of them. This page – these are sketches of two or three instruments of torture that I pictured using on the seminar leader. And underneath those, this is a stab hole I made in the paper with my biro when I realised there were still forty minutes to go and I was stuck in the middle of the front row, so I couldn't walk out. Oh, and here's my note to the Society of Frog Worshippers asking if they exist, and how much it would cost to join.'

'Now, that *is* a good idea, Dad.'

'You think so?'

'I'd jump at it. Geddit? Anyway, Mum says you've got another three lined up.'

'I'd better stick to it. See what happens.'

Saturday, 4 p.m.

Only managed to get to two of the other seminars. The first was delivered by a man who sounded North American and looked like the mountain in *The Waltons*. He was bald on top of his head, with very long grey hair at the back and sides, and a startlingly enormous beard. He delivered his talk from quite a high stage in a massive, barn-like venue attended by a handful of people dotted around the foothills.

Why is it that in an age when many people are – thank

God – trying to abandon or at least cut down on the use of Christianese, others are committedly creating an entirely new and equally impenetrable language with which to puzzle believers and unbelievers alike?

This man announced in prophetic tones that a big part of his mission involved 'triangulating with the sustainer'. I and the other six members of the audience exuded puzzlement.

The two o'clock session was well attended. It was called 'Locating the Deeper Movement of Your Spiritual Narrative'. It was led by a very enthusiastic, mildly bearded man who – would you believe? – had written a book. His boldly expressed central contention was that Christian living is, in a very real sense, as much a matter of bowel as of heart. Left quietly when he reached his third point: 'Assimilation and Evacuation'.

Saturday, 6 p.m.
Back at the chalet, I told Anne and Gerald and Josey about my experiences in the second and third sessions. Caused much amusement.

Gerald said, 'Tell you what, I'm glad we're in a chalet. Just imagine if you found you were camping right next to the man who triangulates with the sustainer in one tent and the bowel man locating his narrative on the other side. I mean, that really could be a longish night.'

Josey nearly fell off her chair laughing.

Asked them about their seminars. Anne said she went to a session called 'Kingdom Kindness', all about the powerful effect of simply being kind to people who need a little care. Very moving and inspiring, she said. Wish I'd gone, but didn't say so.

Gerald went to something called a prophetic workshop in the afternoon. People were asked to take a piece of cloth out of a big box with their eyes closed, and discover what God was saying to them through the nature of the material. His was a scruffy bit of denim with some unpleasant stains on it. He said he threw it away in disgust and walked out, then suddenly burst into tears and spent the rest of the afternoon praying for the people in his church.

Josey took his arm and cuddled him for a moment. Anne looked at me and smiled.

Josey said she truly had meant to go to some seminars, but on the way she met up with a very nice group of people who had decided that coffee and chat and getting to know each other better was just what they needed. Said she wanted me to come along and meet her new friends tomorrow.

Anne tapped something in the programme with her finger and said, 'Unless, of course, Adrian, God calls you to active involvement in tomorrow's exciting Christian Furniture Symposium, an event that is, if it's anything like last year, a time of signs and wonders and miracles – and pulpits.'

'And desks.'

'And lecterns.'

'And hassocks.'

'And plastic stacking chairs.'

All three of them fell about.

I sometimes think I have been placed on this earth solely to offer light relief to Josey and Gerald and Anne – and God.

Josey took my hand and said, 'Miracles are all very well, Adrian, but if you come with me tomorrow, guess what you'll get?'

'What's that, Josey?'

'A doughnut.'

No contest.

Saturday, late evening

Volunteered to stay in and welcome Minnie to the chalet while the others went off to have a drink before dinner. Gerald hung back for a moment as they left. He said, 'Dad, are you really going to do this baring all thing with Minnie when she gets here?'

I said with dignity, 'It is not a "baring all thing", Gerald. I just want to clear the air.'

He did a calming down thing with his hands and said, 'OK. Well, just – be careful. See you both at the meal in a while.'

Minnie arrived soon after that. Helped her get bags and things into her bedroom, then made her a cup of tea. I said, 'Minnie, we'll go over and join the others for dinner in a minute, but before we go, as we're sitting here together, there's something I just need to say to you.'

She did her ghastly tilted head thing and looked at me with soupy compassion.

'Adrian, we're all here rooting for you. God is here for you. Feel free to open your little hurting heart to me.'

'No, no, that's not what I mean. Look, what I mean is that I want to tell you how I really feel about you, and—'

To my horror, she leaned forward, lifted the first and second fingers of her right hand and laid them against my lips.

She said, 'Hush now, Adrian. You know that I love you, but not in a Rachel and Ross sort of way. Nor in a strokey-wokey, whose-turn-is-it-to-make-the-bed sort of way. You are a married man with a lovely-dovely wife. Be a strong little man, Adrian, be strong. Let us leave now. We shall promise each other never to speak of this again. It will be our secret until the very end of time.'

Took her fingers away from my lips at last. Her advice about being strong was very apt. The heavy metal vase that I'd used for discerning some of my seminar choices was inches from my right hand. One vigorous swing would have removed a major obstacle from my life.

I said, 'Minnie, you have completely misunderstood what I was trying to say.'

She gave a horrible conspiratorial wink, and said, 'Of course I have, Adrian. Don't worry. It will be our only-remembered-in-the-middle-of-the-night secret.'

Gave up and went to the restaurant with her. The others were already there.

When Minnie went off to fill her bowl at the salad bar, Anne whispered, 'How did it go?'

I sighed and whispered back, 'Very badly indeed. She thinks I love her in a Rachel and Ross, whose-turn-is-it-to-make-the-bed sort of way, but I have to be a strong little man, and it will be our secret until the end of time.'

Anne laughed so much that she nearly choked on her drink. When she recovered I was going to ask her not to tell Gerald, but she was already whispering in his ear, with Josey craning her neck round to hear what was being said.

Ah, well – they enjoyed the meal, anyway.

Saturday, very late
Feeling much happier. Went to the evening celebration after our meal. Still makes my hair stand on end. Loads and loads of people wanting to somehow be part of the body of Christ despite all their different fears and doubts and

dreams and wonderful experiences and hard-to-understand disappointments. Found myself in tears as we sang a song that starts 'You call me out upon the waters'.

Turned to Anne and whispered, 'What do you think Jesus is thinking?'

She said, 'I think his heart goes out to us.'

Later on, Anne said, 'I did warn you about talking to Minnie, darling. When it comes to you she doesn't seem to ever quite hear what you're saying to her.'

I said, 'I know. You were right. Anne, tell me, do you love me in a whose-turn-is-it-to-make-the-bed sort of way?'

Anne smiled and said, 'Absolutely, sweetheart, and any additional details in that area will remain our secret until the end of time.'

'Thank goodness for that.'

Thought for a moment and said, 'Anne, why do you think God's put Minnie in my life? I mean – almost every encounter I have with her drives me round the bend. I felt like hitting her round the head with a heavy vase earlier on. What's going on?'

Anne yawned. 'Goodness me, what a question at this time of night. Perhaps it's a bit like Paul.'

'Paul who?'

'Paul the apostle. He had a thorn in his flesh, didn't he? To keep him humble. Maybe Minnie's your thorn. People who do great things for God need a thorn, you know.'

'Yes. Yes, I like the sound of that.'

Just dropping off when Anne added, 'So, actually, you should thank God for Minnie.'

Hmm . . .

4

All People Great and Small

Matthew's Gospel says that when Jesus saw the crowds, he had compassion on them because they were harassed and helpless, like sheep without a shepherd (Matt. 9:36). Nowadays, of course, we have sorted all that. In this day and age Christian communities have no reason to feel harassed or helpless. So much support is available. So that's all right, isn't it?

No, it is not. The shepherding task remains, and for anyone who wants to get involved there will never be a shortage of folk who need unharassing (if that's a word – well, it is now), and constructive, non-bullying organisation and help.

Lots of people have been very kind to Bridget and me over the years. We are very grateful.

I guess we all have to take turns being shepherds and sheep. If we accept that and really go for it we shall meet a whole host of different people. It will not always be easy, in either role. After all, when we are harassed and helpless we are not necessarily at our most attractive best. However, change does happen, and the process will continue to be fascinating and instructive and humbling and warming – and occasionally very entertaining.

I could tell you about thousands of real people we have known over the years. Here are just a few of them – oh, and, as you will see, one who is entirely imaginary.

Hazel

I first met Hazel when we were both sixteen years old, and my last conversation with her was on the phone a decade ago, shortly before she went into hospital for the last time. She asked me to pray for her, and on this occasion I did do that, every day until I learned of her death.

Hazel is just one of the many brave survivors we have known, one of those people who face physical and emotional battles of one kind or another every single day. Severely physically handicapped from birth, simply moving around was a painful, laborious business, and events in early life had left her inwardly severely scarred. As a teenager she was bitter and resentful. Anything that I or others said to her about the Christian faith was received with scorn and vitriolic rejection.

After I left home for college in Bristol I hardly saw Hazel for a year or so. Then, one day when I returned to Tunbridge Wells at the end of term, I met her just outside the railway station. Something had happened. There was a light inside her. She smiled at me. There was no vitriol. Only those who had known her previously could even begin to understand the scale of that change. I asked her what had happened.

Hazel told me that she had gone to the morning service at a small Pentecostal Church up on St John's Road. She sat in the back row as far from the front and as near to the door as she could and spoke to no one. At some point during the service she began to experience heat passing right down the length of her body from the top of her head to the bottom of her feet. Nothing else happened, but that heat seemed to have left a residual warmth in her spirit.

Hazel continued to deal with many problems in her life, and certainly faced abysmally dark experiences from time to time, but I know the light that had been put into her was never extinguished. I have never seen such a change in any other person before or since.

Bridget and I dipped in and out of Hazel's life on many occasions over the years, and we never failed to admire the courage with which she tackled obstacles, and the depth of her creative artistry, an instinct that was never quenched by adversity. We wish we could be with her once more, preferably in the Museum Tea Rooms in Hove, Sussex, a place that she loved, and the last place where we met for coffee and cake.

Sadly, I was unable to go to Hazel's funeral. My son Joe kindly took my place and read the poem that follows to those who were gathered there. It is simply called 'Hazel'.

Hazel,
What do I remember?
Cats and giant canvases,
And how to get from A to B.
When L and Q come crashing in to crack the pavement
And release the ancient bears,
Then X intrudes, but not to offer gentle kisses,
Just a sign of getting something wrong.
A little better when the T arrives, a teasing possibility,
That thousands of those tiny photographs might well be
    whispering,
Oh, Hazel, you are beautiful.

Hazel,
What do I remember?
Cats and giant canvases,
And moving from the darkness
Into unexpected, drenching light.
What happened on that puzzling morning?
How I wish I could have seen it,
Alkali from heaven neutralising acid
With such flowing generosity.
Meeting you that day in Tunbridge Wells beside the
    station,
I saw and felt the shocking power of love.
Hazel, you were beautiful.

Hazel,
What do I remember?
Cats and giant canvases,
A secret link
To what it means to make a thing,
And see that it is good.
And yet you understood that all our worlds are works in
    progress,
Colours need to fly until our contribution ends,
And in a place where everything is new and filled with
    love,
The one who truly knows and understands
Will take your hands, and smile, and say,
There, I told you so,
It was as true as blue is truly blue,
Hazel, you are beautiful.

Four People Who Were Gifts from God

I wrote the letter that follows for my website in the autumn of 2015. Some gifts from God were 'unsigned', in the sense that there was no apparent connection with him at the time when they were given. Three of the gifts received through the four people mentioned here were exactly that. It is very easy for the provenance of these gifts to be missed, forgotten or displaced by religious gubbins. The fourth gift was not of the unsigned variety, but writing about our encounter with that particular person was one of the most difficult things I have ever undertaken. As you read it you will understand why.

Dear beloved friends and darling foes,

As I write, October is about to creep in under cover of a thick fog that is enveloping the part of Northern England where we live. I have to confess that I quite enjoy misty mornings. These early autumn days bring a rush of joy as I realise that we are back in the season where a reduction of natural light allows electric lamps to twinkle an increasingly delicious invitation from the little coffee shops that Bridget and I love far too much. The better ones offer coffee and walnut cake as well, of course. And cream teas. And toasted teacakes. And Yorkshire Tea. And lemon drizzle cake. And newspapers you can borrow. All with an appropriate measure of sweet melancholy.

We arrived back home yesterday afternoon after a busy but richly layered weekend at Scargill House. This was our annual event in association with ACW, the Association of Christian Writers. The attendees included published and aspiring writers, many of whom have become good friends, both with us and with each other. This year the theme was 'Heart to Heart', concentrating on the need to write out of truthful experience and to ensure that we are well acquainted with the characters who inhabit our prose fiction or drama.

Our sincere thanks to all who took part. Some memorable pieces were written and read aloud during those three days. Bridget and I marvelled yet again at the depth of talent that is unearthed and revealed when people write out of passion and truth. There was a lot going on, and I suspect that it will go on for much longer in the hearts of those who began their own small but significant voyages of self-discovery in the course of the weekend. Whether it's daffodils or childhood trauma, and in vacant or pensive mood, some processing will almost certainly be required.

Since returning home, Bridget and I have been doing some processing of our own, talking yet again about something that is painfully lodged in our hearts. It is not very easy or comfortable to express.

Let me start by presenting you with a list. There are four people on my list, and they have something in common, beyond the fact that I have written about them all at various times in the past. I suspect that you will very soon identify that common factor. The cause and source of our pain comes from an upcoming event connected with the last of these people. So, here we go.

Number one on my list is someone I shall call Philip. Philip was in the same class as me at junior school. He was what censorious parents used to call 'a rough boy'.

Most of us tended to give him a wide berth.

It happened on another autumn day, when we were about ten years old. On the way home from school across the common, my friends decided to amuse themselves by throwing my school cap into the middle of a dank and dirty pond just outside the village. We called it the Marl Pit. My cap sat flatly upon a small, downtrodden patch of reeds sticking up in the middle, way out of reach. Naturally, I pretended to find the whole thing funny, but inside I wanted to cry. If I arrived home without my cap there would be big trouble.

Philip, passing by on his own, was drawn by all the hilarity. Realising what was going on, he ran to his nearby house and returned quite quickly wearing wellingtons. Wading into the water with a length of dead branch in his hands, he eventually retrieved my headwear and passed it to me without comment. Perhaps he had sensed, for a short time at least, that we were brothers in alienation.

The bond did not last long. I was momentarily grateful, but mostly all too happy just to be one of the gang again. Philip trudged off alone towards his home.

I saw almost nothing of Philip after junior school. We went our separate ways, I to grammar school and he to the local secondary modern. Later, I heard that he had become involved in violent crime, eventually spent time in prison and died at an early age, racked with depression and illness. Nobody had a good word to say for him.

He got my cap back for me.

Second on my list is a man whose name I shall never know. He was a porter at a London railway station, in the days when such people existed and were available. I was about fifteen, and as green as they come. This gentleman helped me to carry my collection of unwieldy bags (some things don't change, do they?) to a bus stop outside the station. I was vaguely aware that porters needed to be given some sort of tip as a reward for their services, so I took two two-shilling pieces from my pocket and placed them into his hand. He studied the pair of coins for a second or two, then raised his eyes to look into mine. For a moment I assumed that I'd got it wrong. Perhaps four shillings was not enough. Before I could react or say a word, he picked one of the coins out of his palm, handed it back to me and hurried away in the direction of the station.

I had never seen this man before and, as far as I know, I have never come across him again. In fact, I know only one thing about him.

When I was young and naïve, he showed me kindness and generosity.

Number three was a man who worked at the paint distribution warehouse where I had a holiday job in the mid-1970s. I was at teacher training college in Bromley, and for Bridget and me and our one-year-old son, Matthew, money was short. This was not helped by the fact that we were still both smokers, and the grinding tedium of assembling paint orders for eight endless hours each day was relieved only by the occasional cigarette. Watching paint dry is popularly supposed to be the apogee of boredom, but only by those who have never assembled trolley-load after trolley-load of glosses and emulsions in the dank canyons of a paint-infested universe.

One morning I forgot to take my cigarettes to work. I

had no money to buy any more. All I had was my return bus ticket. I was devastated. How on earth was I going to survive an entire day of unremitting, paint-related toil without cigarettes to break the monotony?

George, a fellow employee who had perfected the art of only appearing to our boss on rare occasions, as he pushed his trolley with increased speed and thespian zeal past the far end of one of those eternal canyons, noticed during our morning break that I was not smoking. I explained that I had left them on the hall table at home. He said next to nothing in response, but from that moment until the end of the day he found me at regular intervals to give me a cigarette from his packet.

George was a quiet, stolid, unambitious man in his late forties. He had been at the warehouse for years, and, as far as one could tell, might have continued to push paint around until the end of his working life. I think he watched a great deal of television on his own at home, but that's about all I do know, apart from this one ineradicable fact.

He noticed that I was unhappy, and he did something about it.

And so we come to the fourth person on our list, and the reason that Bridget and I are experiencing such pain at the moment. We encountered this man during our involvement in a radio discussion series that very enjoyably punctuated our work with children in care in the first half of the 1980s. I'll call him John. John was about fifteen years older than us, a widely experienced minister of the Church who, through his own charismatic personality and gently loving ways, introduced us to a

God who was and is less judgemental, less pointlessly religious and far more of a warm friend than the frowning deity that we had cobbled together in our minds and spirits since the days when we first believed. John's God was nice. He never forgot you. He was far more eager to mend and improve his relationship with us than we were. John's God was not soft, but he was safe, and quietly determined that we would not be lost to the more negative sides of ourselves. It was a revelation. A burst of sunshine in a dull and lightless day.

The understanding and appreciation of God that was gifted to us by John during those few short years has become the bedrock of our faith, and we shall always be grateful for the privilege of having known him. He cleaned the windows of our perception, allowing a flood of light to enter.

In a few months from now, years since we knew him, we have learned that John will have to face accusations which, if proved, will take him into a very dark place. We have no argument with that process. Where there is excessive wrongdoing there needs to be exposure and appropriate punishment. Our pain is caused by the car crash of a collision in our hearts between the channel of peace that John undoubtedly was in the years that we knew him and the person who may well have been guilty of crimes that we find utterly abhorrent.

Nobody is one thing. Not one of us is purely good or purely evil. The image of a man quietly drawing in the dust as a woman waits to be stoned to death must always constrain us from self-indulgent or defensive judgement of others. The four people on my list have in common their willingness to give gifts to me and, in the case of John, to Bridget as well, and to many other people. The gifts that these individuals gave were real and true and good, whatever has happened in the rest of their lives, and if there is ever to be a place where a final reckoning is made, I shall be obliged, a little nervous and (I hope) happy to mention them.

I may be a bit confused at times, but I do know a cup of water when I see one.

My best to all of you,
Yours sincerely, Adrian

Wooden Man

We pay lip-service to the notion that no one can earn their way into heaven, but conversations with many Christians suggest that they are still firmly in the grip of a law whose demands in their view will inevitably slam the door shut on failure. Maybe I was one of them once. Not any more. I know now that we are all failures, so it is just as well that the law no longer calls the shots. Sadly, I have learnt that many Christians take a lot of convincing about this. Sometimes it is through a sort of inverted pride, a stubborn, even quite militant, refusal to give up the right to decide on their own worthiness. Sometimes it is a genuine problem for those whose sense of self-value has been seriously crushed by personal experience.

A: All I can think about is how rotten I am inside. There seem to be so *many* sins. When you get rid of one, another one pops up to take its place. I don't think I'll ever be good enough to do anything really useful for God. I know nobody's perfect but . . .

B: Well, now you mention it, nobody except my friend Richard. He's never committed a sin in his life.

A: There isn't anyone who hasn't done anything wrong – is there?

B: My friend Richard hasn't.

Pause.

A: He's never done anything wrong? A perfect Christian?

B: My friend Richard – he's never stolen, never murdered, never committed adultery, never envied, never lusted, never told a single lie, never been guilty of a cowardly act, never hurt anyone, never hit anyone, never hustled, harassed or hated anyone—

A: But surely—

B: Richard – honestly – he's never been greedy, thoughtless or avaricious, he's never dropped litter, disturbed the peace, driven with excess alcohol in his blood or destroyed other people's property. He's never had a single unkind thought, he holds no grudges, he never gossips, he's never late or lascivious or libellous. He has never caused, continued or condoned conflict of any kind. He never complains, he never blasphemes, he never gets drunk, he never overeats, he worships no false images, he's never mean or menacing or malicious.

A: But isn't that—?

B: Richard never watches nasty videos, nor does he condemn people who do; he's never judgemental or oversentimental or harsh or unforgiving. He's never sad, bad or mad. He never smokes, he never swears, he's never rude, he never stares. Richard has never ever committed a single sin. Oh, and one other thing.

A: What's that?

B: He won't be going to heaven.

A: I'm not surprised. He's not likely to be very good company, is he?

B: No, no, it's because – well, tell you what, do you want to meet him?

A: Ye-e-e-s. I suppose. When?

B: Now. Hold on. He's in my pocket.

A: What?!

B: There you are. Look. He's a little tiny wooden man. I made him. And he won't be going to heaven because he's made of wood.

A: Yes, but hold on. That's not fair on little – Richard. You said – you said he was a perfect Christian.

B: No, I didn't – you said that. I just told you about all the things he's never done wrong. The trouble with little – good old Richard is that although he's never committed any of the sins I was talking about, he's never done anything else either. He can't. He's made of wood. So . . .

A: So?

B: So, it doesn't matter if you don't do anything wrong for the rest of your life. It won't make you a Christian and it won't get you into heaven.

A: (*pause*) So, what will then?

B: Now *that* is another question altogether.

Snapshots from Israel

A few years ago we visited the Holy Land for the first time. We became very fond of the group that we were helping to lead, and simply being in that part of the world was a truly memorable, complicated experience. Here are just three snapshots from that trip.

Snapshot one

We are sitting on some steps, purpose-built for tourists and pilgrims, overlooking a narrow, sluggishly flowing strip of brown water. Camera-clicking groups from at least four other nations surround us. They all seem very excited to find themselves here.

I ask myself if this can really be the Jordan. My mental picture of the famous river has been expanded and perhaps exaggerated by its significance in various parts of the Bible. The passages that immediately spring to mind at this moment, however, concern Naaman, army commander to the king of Aram, who was told by the prophet Elisha to bathe seven times in the Jordan if he wanted to be healed of his skin disease. I think Naaman must have taken a look at Israel's muddy river because he decided that Abana and Pharpar, beautifully clear waters in his home region of Damascus, would be a much better bet.

He changed his mind about that in the end, fortunately for himself and for those who cared about him, but I see his point. A plunge into that turgid stream looks as if it might do more harm than good.

Fortunately, I do not mention my negative reflections, because others in our group are convinced, each for their own particular reasons, that baptism in the River Jordan is exactly what they need – and they are absolutely right. Tears fill my eyes as, one after another, those willing souls disappear for an eternal two seconds beneath the opaque surface, reappearing with expressions on their faces that I will not attempt to define.

Equally moving is the way in which two members of our group set aside any denominational or theological differences in order to perform the act of baptism for those who stepped into the water. Finally, these two men, both great assets to our group in many ways, wrestle each other under the water, disappearing like very amateur synchronised swimmers, and pop up again moments later with wide beams across their dripping faces.

The Jordan has been there for a very long time, but it seems that the Holy Spirit is still available for individual encounters down among the fishes.

Snapshot two

Some of the people in our group have problems with mobility.

I am one of them. However, there is an abundance of support and patience among my travelling companions. And most of the time, the desire to see everything possible on a trip that may never be repeated drives me on. Every now and then, however, I have had enough. This is one of those moments: it is time to fall down or find a seat. The latter is preferable, and as the others enter a building which purportedly houses the tomb of Lazarus, I decide to rest my aching back and take a seat on a low wall. Opposite I note the 'Lazarus Souvenir Shop', presumably not an establishment that was available to the little Bethany family Jesus loved to visit.

Next to me on the wall sits a man, his body, legs and arms twisted and misshapen. Beside him stands a cardboard container filled with what appear to be brightly coloured bookmarks with a vaguely Christian theme. A written sign asks for 'donations' from those who would like to help themselves from his box. I introduce myself and ask what his name is.

He smiles and replies in quite clear English, 'My name is Zid.'

I assume that this is a slight mispronunciation.

'Ah,' I prattle, 'Sid is an English name, short for Sidney.'

'No, no, it is Z-z-zid.' He buzzes out the first letter to make sure that I have heard correctly. 'And Zid is short for William.'

I am disconcerted by this piece of apparent misinformation, but I like Zid. He is a very friendly man. I point to his box.

'And these are things that you sell?'

'Not sell. Just donations. My uncle makes them for me.'

'I see. And are you a Christian, Zid?'

'No. I am Muslim.'

'Can I ask you a question?'

'Of course.'

You are Muslim, but you and many other Muslims here in Bethany and other places are selling Christian stuff all the time to tourists. Does that – well, does it matter?'

The lopsided smile with which Zid receives this question is a strange mixture of sadness and compassion. I suppose he can see that I am a foreigner who knows nothing.

'What you have to understand,' he says gently, 'is that we are *very* poor.'

In the silence that follows I begin to feel a little lost. Then I think of something.

'Zid,' I say, 'you are Muslim and I am Christian. Can I tell you some words written by a Muslim poet called Jelaludin Rumi, hundreds of years ago?'

'Yes, of course.'

'He wrote something like, "Out beyond ideas of wrong-doing and rightdoing, there is a field. I'll meet you there." Perhaps you and I could meet there one day.'

Zid nods amicable agreement. 'It's a deal.'

Before leaving, I extend a hand towards my new friend. He lifts his distorted arm with some effort, shakes my hand and continues to grip my hand firmly for a moment.

'That field,' he says, 'when we meet there, will you bring me something?'

'Yes, of course I will. Anything that's allowed. What would you like?'

I am very curious. What kind of very special gift does Zid want me to bring along to our encounter in the mystical future?

'A big bar of Cadbury's milk chocolate. Could you bring me that?'

We both laugh.

'Yes,' I say, 'if it's at all possible I promise I will do my very best to bring you a very large bar of Cadbury's chocolate. Goodbye, Zid.'

Later I am afflicted with a sense of sadness and frustration. If Jesus had been sitting beside Zid he would have forgiven the poor man's sins and healed his body. Those

twisted limbs would have been straightened and strength-
ened. I did think about offering to pray for him at the time,
but faith and courage drained away. The words would not
come out of my mouth. Shame. I wish they had. But I am
also glad that they did not. The truth always sets us free,
and sometimes it is wonderful. At other times it is not easy
to live with our use of that freedom.

I hope God will make it possible for me to meet Zid in
that field one day. Is there chocolate in heaven?

A voice whispers, 'Anything is possible – even chocolate.'

Snapshot three

We have been fortunate enough to encounter a wonderful
English guide at the peaceful Garden Tomb in Jerusalem, who
gently puts to rest the turbulent confusion created in some of
our party by learning that incidents of vital importance might
have happened in one of a variety of conflicting sites.

'He may have been buried here,' she says, 'or he may not.
But it doesn't really matter, because the most important
thing is that he has risen.'

Hundreds of thousands, probably millions, of people
come to the Holy Land every year looking for Jesus. The
experience is wonderful, confusing, alarming, exciting,
inspiring and profoundly educational, but our guide is
absolutely right. The Holy Spirit is here and everywhere,
but the crucified man is not, thank God. He has risen.

The Growing-up Pains of Simon Peter

*For me, writing has a lot to do with curiosity. I am, for
instance, genuinely intrigued to discover what might*

happen if I were to have a drink with Simon Peter in a heavenly pub. Of course, I have some idea of the direction the conversation is likely to take. I never go anywhere without views, prejudices and at least a couple of sturdy hobby horses. Such a burden.

The exciting thing, though, is that eavesdropping has a strangely cleansing effect on perception. I sometimes seem to step aside from my own thought processes and find that when the two of us are reunited we have both had to change our minds. A bewildering experience. Here is an example.

I have a number of long-term ambitions connected with my eternal stay in heaven. I'll tell you about one of them now. For this hope to be realised there will have to be a public house just down the street from where my mansion is located. Bright as the lit end of a chunky cigar on a dark but heavenly autumn evening, that glowing home from home will be an ideal venue for intimate chats with individuals who fascinated me but were not around in my time. I'm not sure how specific time-planning is going to work in an environment that is likely to be bewilderingly fluid, but this particular ambition of mine is to experience an encounter with Simon Peter on my very first visit to the local hostelry.

Indulgently embedded in a cosy corner of the bar, my hope is that the big fisherman and I will dip our thrice-fried chips in the ketchup and sip our Harvey's Best Bitter (hopefully, in that home of miracles all favourites will be on tap from an automatically refilled barrel), and I shall at last be able to ask the questions I have stored up for so long. I really can almost imagine how that conversation might go.

ADRIAN: Thanks. Nice ale.

PETER: Mmmm! (*nodding ecstatically and flicking froth away from his hairy chin*) Strong, nutty and room temperature.

A: Excellent! Good. Oh, just a thought, Peter – not forgotten your keys?

P: (*playfully pretends to shoot me with a pistol*) Good one! (*we both laugh uproariously*)

A: (*after a companionable pause*) So, Peter, as you probably know I've only just arrived up here in, er . . .

P: Heaven?

A: Yes. (*glancing around*) Heaven. Thing is, I'm so glad you're here tonight because there's something I've been wanting to ask you for a very long time. I thought I might never get the chance. But here we are! Thing is, it's a bit – well – it is a bit personal. Do you mind?

P: Course not. Fire away.

A: OK. Here goes. You know that time when Jesus said you were going to be the rock he'd build his church on?

P: Mm! Yes. Remember that. It came just after he'd asked us disciples if we were going to clear off like everyone else. I said something like, 'Clear off to where? We want to know how to live forever. You're the one with all the answers.' He seemed well chuffed with that.

A: Well chuffed?

P: (*pleased but slightly embarrassed*) Ah, yeah, just a little expression I picked up here in the pub last week. Good, isn't it? Chuffed! Well *chuffed*! He was well *chuffed*!

A: Mm. Right. Anyway, here's my question. Hearing the stuff about being the rock, how did it – well – how did it make you feel?

P: Mm. Good question. (*nods slowly*) Weird. It was weird. I mean – good, in a way. To be chosen and all that to be a – rock. I have to be honest, though. I had very little idea what he was talking about, and I didn't feel much more like a rock after he said it than before. (*wriggles his shoulders*) Tried to square my shoulders and look a bit more like a – well, some kind of rock, but, no, I didn't feel like that.

A: What did you feel like?

P: Er . . . (*considers*) I think I felt like – a marshmallow.

A: You can't have done. You didn't have marshmallows in your day – did you?

P: No, but I've had some since coming here. Tried loads of things since coming here. (*rubs his hands together*) Been a lot of fun! But, yes, that's what I felt like. Soft. Squishy. Like a marshmallow. (*makes a wobbling movement with his hand*) Kinda – wobbly. (*thinks for a moment*) Thing about it was, though – I don't know if you'll understand this – whenever he told one of us we were something or other that didn't make any sense at all, on some level we sort of automatically believed it.

A: Because it was him who said it, you mean?

P: (*waves a finger*) Exactly! Because he was the one who said it. I mean – I remember, for instance, at our last meal with him before he went to – you know. After we finished eating, he looked round the table, very serious, and he said one of us was going to rat on him. Betray him. Well, we all got upset. I remember whispering to John to ask which of us it was. Comparing notes afterwards, all but one of us were obviously wondering if we might be the one. (*putting his pint down and raising his hands in emphasis*) Well, he'd said it! So . . . (*pause*) Course, one of us – one of us knew he was the one. You know who it was, don't you? (*another pause, before continuing quietly*) And let's face it, later on – as you probably know, pretty much everybody does – it was me as well.

A: (*briskly, after a decent pause*) Right. So, going back to you hearing you were lined up to be a rock – sorry, I mean *the* rock – what happened after that?

P: Lots of stuff. (*shifting uneasily*) I suppose I might have got a bit carried away by the whole thing. I sort of got this idea that maybe I could do things for him – fix things – me being the rock and all.

A: It went a bit wrong, did it?

P: (*nods sadly*) Just a bit, yes. You could say that. (*leaning forward*) You've probably read about it already. You haven't had to put up with knowing there's a book around explaining in detail what an idiot you made of yourself during three years of your life, have you?

A: (*after a moment's thought*) Well, actually, I have in a way . . . Go on, tell me. I want to hear it from you.

P: (*a little surprised*) Oh. Well, anyway, most of the things I tried to do for him before and after that were ridiculous at best and seriously bad ideas at worst. (*silence*) You want to hear the list, don't you?

A: Only if—

P: All right! No, it's all right. All right. In no particular order. Where shall I start? Ah, yes. The time on the mountain. What you would call the Transfiguration. Right. A chance for me to shine – not. We get to the top, quite a long way, hoping to have a bit of a rest, and I'm so overcome by Jesus turning into a human torch (he's the only one who did shine, by the way), and Moses and Elijah with him, two spiritual giants turning up, as spiritual giants do, that I try to help out by offering to build places they can stay in. But why did I say it? Build with what? I had no tools. No materials. There was no wood. I just drivelled on about the first thing that came into my head. I was terrified. Well, done, Rock! Brilliant.

A: Yes, but you weren't to know—

P: Moving on. Another time. Quite a bit later on. He tries to wash my feet. *Him* washing *my* feet. Course, I say, 'NO!' and go all pompous and fake humble, thinking he'll appreciate my example to the others. He looks me straight in the eye and he tells me very seriously that I can't have anything to do with him if I don't let him wash my feet. So, what do I do then? 'Yes! Yes! Yes!' Start shouting like a five-year-old about wanting to be washed all over, not just my feet but all over. (*shaking his head*) I tell you – I go bright red just thinking about it.

A: But surely—

P: And we can't leave out the classic one, can we? Unbelievable! What do I do? Listen to this. Just after he's called me the Rock, I only take the Son of God on one side to talk a bit of sense into him, don't I? To rebuke him. Hmm? To tell him off. The Rock, the foundation of the Church, sorting things out. I told him straight. 'Forget all this stuff about dying,' I said. 'It's not going to happen. I shall personally ensure that you will live a long and happy life.'

A: He wasn't impressed.

P: No, he was not impressed. Not pleased. It was grim, actually. He called me names – well, one name. The whole point, the point I hadn't understood, the point I couldn't get my thick head round, was that he would have *loved, loved, loved, loved* to lead a long and happy life cooking fish and telling stories and all the rest of it. Obviously I didn't get it at the time, but what it amounts to is that I was actually trying to sensibly, reasonably, kindly talk him out of saving the world. Aaah! Imagine that! Satan using the newly appointed Rock to smash the thing that was supposed to be built on him. (*shaking his head in disbelief*) Irony or what?

A: Look, you don't need to go on with—

P: One of the toughest things. I'll tell you about it. (*wrestling with the memory*) One day he sat me down. Just him and me. Close together, facing each other. And I have to say, he talked to me like a real friend. He could do that. He could be a holy terror as well, I tell you. But not this time. Quite – gentle, actually. But the things he said – well, they turned my innards round inside me. He told me Satan wanted to sift me. Like wheat. Would you believe it. Me! I couldn't see why I'd need sifting. I was strong. I was sure. I'd never let him down.

That's what I thought. I really did think that. (*pauses, remembering*) He said he'd pray for my faith to hold out. And I'd got to strengthen my brothers after I came back from wherever I was going. Told him straight. I'm not going anywhere. I am going to look after you.

And you know what? He looked really sad. Really *sad*. Spoke quite quietly. 'Peter, my friend,' he said, 'you are going to betray me three times before the cock crows.'

And it filled me up with panic. Betray him? I couldn't see it. Trouble was – he'd said it. He'd said it. Rock? Blancmange cube, I was. Horrible feeling.

A: (*quietly*) What was it like in the garden?

P: Oh, yes. The garden. Gethsemane. What happened when three of us went along with him to Gethsemane? Support, that's what we were there for.

I don't know about the others, but I knew that was my role. Strong, committed supporter. So what do I do? I fall asleep. Twice. The snoring Rock. He was very upset. *Very* upset. He was very hurt. And in the middle of it, believe it or not, worried about us falling apart. (*stares into the distance for a moment, lost in the memory*) He was in such a state that night. In pieces. No word of a lie – sweating blood. I'd never seen him like that before. Never seen anyone like that.

And then, later, that same night, when the b . . . when they came to arrest him, I was wide awake and now was my big chance to show that I really meant it when I said I'd look after him. I pulled my sword out to defend him and lashed out. Terrible aim. Ended up slicing off this bloke's ear. Five seconds later, the bloke's got a new ear.

'Put your sword away. I don't need it. There are a thousand angels on full alert. I don't need them either.'

Didn't need my sword. Didn't need me. I just stared at him. Froze for a moment. Then I cleared off into the dark.

And, as the entire world now knows, he was right about the other stuff too. Down in the courtyard, three times I found myself bawling and shouting about him being nothing to do with me. I don't know him! I don't *know* him! I've never spoken to him. Why would I want to follow that loser?

Then that cockerel started up. Could've wrung its neck. (*pause*) He turned his head and looked at me.

A: (*softly*) How did that feel?

P: I burst into tears. Ran like a rabbit. The rock he was planning to build his church on was a blubbering wreck down in the shadows by the gate. (*waving a hand*) Oh, don't worry. It's all in the past – if the past exists any more. And, unbelievably, and I mean unbelievably, it worked out fine in the end.

A: Yes. Yes, it did, didn't it? So, what made the difference – in the end, I mean?

P: Another good question. (*after serious thought*) What he'd done was, he'd made me put all my usual weapons down. Every single one. Made me redundant. That nearly finished me off. I wasn't – anything. But I know now: he had to do that. And later on, after he stopped being dead, he cooked some fish for me on the seashore. That was nice. Very nice. Asked if I loved him. Three times. Said I did. Three times. He asked me to help him. I said I would. (*pauses*) It was true. I did love him. Still do. (*smiles*) Always will. Forever.

A: Another pint?

P: (*raising his glass*) Why not? One more Harvey's. Best ale in the Angler's Rest.

A: Oh! That's odd. I could have sworn the sign outside said it was called the Writer's Block.

P: *He'd* call it the Carpenter's Arms.

A: Why the—? Ah! Of course. (*thinks for a moment*) Interesting. What do other people say it's called? John the Baptist, what does he call it?

P: J the B? J the B calls it the King's Head. (*laughs and adds contentedly*) Good one, eh? Whatever you call it – it's heaven. Go on, get the drinks in.

A: Right. (*pauses, unsure, and pats his pockets*) Oh. I never thought. Do I need money here?

P: (*leans back and smiles*) Money? Good Lord, no. Everything's paid for.

In Two Minds – Jesus and the Syrophoenician Woman

I wish I could have been a silent witness in the corner when Jesus and the passionately needy mother from Syrophoenicia met. My personal interpretation of what we do know about this encounter is a good example of the way in which one's view can change. Even now, I am not sure if I totally agree with myself about some of the conclusions I seem to have drawn in that context, and you may have a completely different view again.

Then there will be three of us involved in the argument. I would look forward to that.

With a sigh of relief, Jesus enters the house of a generous supporter in the city of Tyre, hoping against hope that his arrival has not been noticed. He is racked with tiredness after dealing with the crowds of people who constantly petition him for help and healing. He has always been vividly, almost painfully, conscious of power going out of him for the healing of just one person. Focusing on and dealing with the needs of hundreds has left him drained and seriously in need of a place to rest and find new strength. This house, on this day, might offer him exactly what he needs.

It is not to be.

Moments after leaning his back against a satisfying, Saviour-shaped hollow in the wall and allowing his eyes to close at last, his senses tell him that another person has entered the room. Raising his eyelids a fraction of an inch, he discovers that a woman is kneeling in front of him. Her clothes and manner betray her origin immediately. She is not of the Jewish people.

Opening his eyes wide and looking directly into her face, he sees intelligence, awareness and a burning passion, contained for the moment but almost certainly about to be expressed in words.

For a moment, his heart sinks. He knows who this is. Earlier, he felt decidedly disinclined to meet or offer help to the woman. But what is temptation for, if not to be resisted? The moment passes. Deep breath. Encounters like this are part of the reason for his coming, and, in any case, there is something about her that appeals to him on more than one level. He smiles a little at his own thoughts, leaning forward so that his elbows rest on his knees, his fingers steepled beneath his chin.

'Tell me.'

The story flies out of her in a shapeless storm. The unclean spirit. The demented girl. The horror. The heartbreak. The sudden hope. The journey. The decision to make a plea for help. The determination to enter this house on her own, driven by love and fear.

He listens, nodding gently as she speaks. There is more than a hint of mutual understanding in the meeting of their eyes. Unconditional love, passion, determination, a keen wit, perhaps. If true, these are all things they have in common.

'And perhaps, as a Gentile, you would care to explain to me,' he says in response, still with a smile on his lips, one eyebrow raised quizzically, 'why you suppose that I might be willing to take the children's food and throw it – to the dogs?'

She does not disappoint him. For the first time there is a glimmer of light in her expression. Collecting herself, she holds his gaze steadily with her own.

'Because, sir,' she replies, 'even the dogs eat the scraps that the children happen to drop under the table. Is that not so?'

He chuckles quietly in appreciation.

'Yes, yes, indeed they do. Well said. Very well said. You should go home now. Look after your daughter. She is waiting for you. Very excited to see you.' A pause. 'She is well.'

After the woman has left, weeping tears of happiness, he leans back, smiles for a moment or two, then closes his tired eyes once more and asks for another layer of strength. He knows all too well what will happen now. It is a pattern in his life. This relieved mother's emotional exit from the house will not go unnoticed. Soon – all too soon – there will be others.

5

Blessed Be Scargill

Since its reopening early in 2010, Bridget and I have been closely and gratefully involved with Scargill House, situated among the beautiful, honey-glazed hills of Yorkshire. Scargill is home to an intentional Christian community and is run as a retreat, holiday and conference centre. Our current home is a two-hour drive north of the centre, but contact has carried on to the present day through close friendships and regular involvement in teaching events.

The grim experiences of the Covid pandemic of 2020–21 hit the Scargill Community in ways that are directly related to its identity. The organisation exists not just for its live-in members, but also for the benefit of large numbers of regular guests and newcomers who were unable to visit during the extensive periods of lockdown restrictions that we all endured. In the past the duty of caring for the varied needs of their guests has always given community members a means of safely testing and exploring the depth and authenticity of their spiritual development.

Predictably, the excellent leadership team rose to the occasion, overcoming many obstacles to survival. Scargill is very much alive, and determined not to die.

The process of bringing Scargill House back to life more than a decade ago also raised its own particular set of challenges, discoveries and reflections. In the ongoing context of coronavirus they might acquire a fresh force. See what you think.

Bridget and I were quite sure that we were intended to be a small part of the resurrection of Scargill House. We knew there would be problems and obstacles on the way, but if we had not been unusually confident that God thought it was the right place for us to be we might have given up at a very early stage. In those first months, as I am sure all those involved would agree, nobody was quite sure exactly what Scargill was to become, or how that was to be achieved. Little wonder that occasional dark moments introduced challenges we could not have anticipated.

The Gift of Devastation

There was an interesting moment back near the very beginning of Scargill's new life. It happened during a meeting in the beautiful George Pace designed chapel, set high above the rest of the buildings. Those present were invited to speak to God, either silently or aloud. A young man sitting at the end of the front pew near the exit stood up. In the course of his prayer he said something strange. He asked God to send devastation to Scargill.

There are times when an image or a sound or a few words seem to throw themselves at my attention and refuse to move on. This was such a time. But what could his prayer mean? The suggestion that Scargill should welcome devastation was not echoed by many of us. Not surprising, really. Why on earth would we welcome devastation? Yet I remained convinced of its importance, even though I had scant understanding of what I was convinced about.

As Scargill's new existence began to take on some kind of rough shape, we discovered the truth of this prayer, and the depth of its significance. Devastation was to be exactly what we got.

Lessons learned over the following years proved to be valuable beyond measure. Like Solomon after the light disappeared from his newly built temple, we discovered that the pattern of God keeping his promise about being in the cloud can be repeated. Some moments brought tears to our eyes. We found ourselves encountering so many visitors (and a number of Community members) who brought dysfunction, disappointment and confusion into our willing but inexpert and uncertain embrace.

In hindsight, the devastation they brought with them was a gift to us. Clearly, our task was to accept and embrace, without too much fuss, the pain and darkness they carried. Crucially, we resolved to avoid pummelling them with that thing called 'ministry', a facility that can be more useful to insensitive 'ministers' than to the ministered-to. That determination to avoid inflicting unhelpful pressure is still an important feature of Scargill's hospitality, but I know many in the Community from then until the present day would acknowledge a multitude of mistakes.

There was so much to learn. It was truly alarming to discover that pain, revelation, conflict and relief could all be wrapped up in a single, educational package.

The pain could be horrible. The revelation was sometimes profound and often deeply helpful. Occasional conflicts along the way were wounding but perhaps inevitable.

The story is a familiar one. Crucifixion hurts. Resurrection is hard to handle. The story continues. It must. Devastation continues to be a welcome guest at Scargill House.

Working Friends

From the very beginning we were meeting people from all over the world who would challenge our thinking. Some would enter our hearts. Among these were members of the Community, guests and volunteers. Two of the latter group (now known as Working Friends), a man and a woman whom we met soon after we arrived, had a profound impact on Bridget and me, although both would have considered themselves insignificant as contributors to Scargill's forward motion.

Paul was an older man filled with quirks and flaws and sweetness. He came regularly and worked very hard on the estate team. Paul was not a very confident Christian, but he was a true believer and he often had important questions that needed answering.

One day, as I walked down the drive to our cottage, I came across my friend fiercely digging up something or other. I liked Paul. It was always a pleasure to chat with him. He stopped, leaned on his spade and hitched his hat up on his forehead.

'Adrian, if you've got a moment, would it be all right if I asked you a question?'

'Yes, of course.'

'The thing is,' he said, a little hesitantly, 'I'm – well, I'm not that good at praying and stuff like that. I just wondered what you thought about something I've thought I might do.'

I was intrigued. Paul often surprised me with new ideas.

'The thing is,' he said, 'I reckoned I might offer God each of the jobs I do here as a sort of prayer. So, I mean – I'd say,

"Here you are, God. This is for Jim." Something like that. Do you think that would go down OK as a prayer?'

Not many people are genuinely original.

'Paul,' I said, 'I wish I'd thought of that. It's a fantastic idea.'

He smiled, tugged his hat down and returned to his digging.

Then there was Irene, whose prayers for Scargill were legendary, a lady who represented the very best of selfless commitment to a cause in which she passionately believed. Her death was painfully bad news for everyone who knew her.

This poem, written in her memory, is partly inspired by a sudden glimpse of Irene on the hillside at the back of Scargill House. Behind her, the early evening sun, an intense silver light, blazed through the brilliant white hair that framed her face. It was as though she was wearing a halo.

Of course, it never was a bona fide halo,
More a trick of light.
Summer sunshine streams like water down the limestone
    slopes of Scargill.
Irene happened to adopt her everyday aesthetic-academic
    pose,
Between that shining river and my captivated eyes.
Just her white and startling hair ignited from behind,
Leaving one forever snapshot on the hope-detecting
    surface of my memory.
Of course, it can't have been a halo, can it?
Probably the product of an unfamiliar light.
Who, in this dark challenge of a world, could ever claim
    a halo?

Not Irene,

Not the person she would sometimes dare to view, like
some small, nervous child,

Through the troubled, misty lens of self-examination.

No. You, and him, and her, and them, the ones she loved,

And even those who showed no sign of loving her,

These were haloed, sometimes to their own surprise,

By the sparkling spray or shower of her unrestrained
humility.

No, it never was a halo.

Possibly a revelation of our own deep need,

The yearning you and I have for a promise or a sign,

That treasure stored in heaven, the currency of loving
hearts,

Will never fade or fail.

One day we shall see and know the truth of that.

But in the meantime, God says, 'She is here, and she is
mine,

Her heart is rich, her life with me and those she loves is
drenched with light and peace,

And, oh, my goodness, you should see her halo shine.'

The Meal, Not the Recipe

*Purely theoretical Christianity can provide a very attractive
and convincing alternative to real engagement, but it tends
to result in containment rather than freedom. We are only
just beginning to understand what that might involve.*

Experiences at Scargill taught us how important it is to
smile at people. Sounds obvious, doesn't it?

One of the most captivating things about being a stumbling, faltering follower of Jesus like me is the realisation that it involves offering a genuine smile to people in situations where they least expect it. Broad smiles can be amazingly effective, but as I naturally veer more towards the basilisk end of the smile spectrum, it is just as well that sharing the smile of God does not have to be a facial expression. It can apply in all sorts of situations. It could be a garden sorted out for a beleaguered friend. It could be the provision of a well providing clean water for a small community in the slums of Bangladesh. It could be an hour spent with a lonely, elderly person. It might be an anonymous gift or unexpected forgiveness or a temporary abandonment of the rules or telling a benevolent lie to your brother about the fact that you don't really want the last sausage so he might as well have it. Or just keeping your mouth shut for once.

All these things and many more besides are regular features in the lives of Christians who are more interested in being Jesus in the world than merely talking about him. And yes, of course it is true that many, many non-Christians are continually involved in acts of love. What is the difference?

There is only one source of love, whoever you are and whatever you believe. Those who have embarked on the difficult, fascinating, confusing, hope-filled path of Christian living hope and believe that we have discovered the wellspring of love, however and wherever it is expressed.

Words are needed occasionally, and smiles that come from the heart are wonderful, but bona fide love offers a meal, not a recipe.

Imagine guests have come to your house for dinner.

Ushered to the table by you, they discover a recipe carefully laid out for each of them.

'It's a perfect meal!' you enthuse. 'The best vegetables, and a really good cut of meat. All the instructions are there, so just take the recipe home with you and use it with our love. Have a wonderful time and do let us know how it goes. Bless you!'

Every now and then we meet disappointed, slightly bewildered Christians who are wondering why things have failed to work out in the way they had hoped. Recipes galore, but nothing on the plate. Perhaps these yearning prodigals need to have a word with whoever waylaid them as they headed for home. The conversation might go something like this:

ELDER: Good morning. I gather you wanted to see me. How are you?

PRODIGAL: Fine, thanks. Well, sort of. Yes, I did want to see you. I just wanted to let you know that – oh, dear, there's no other way to say this – I've decided to leave. Before I go, though, I'd just like to thank you for greeting me so warmly and enthusiastically when I first turned up. The thing is—

E: Oh! The things that happened when you arrived were just wonderful, weren't they? All the gifts. The cloak? The ring? The sandals? The fatted calf? The great party? The Father's total forgiveness!

P: Ye-e-s. Yes, about those things.

E: What? You didn't enjoy them?

P: Er, well, yes, I did – in a way.

E: In a way?

P: It was overwhelming. I mean, one minute I was making my way hopefully but rather miserably towards home, the next you appeared and offered me all those things. I couldn't believe it. I thought – I've done it! I've made it! It was fantastic.

E: Right, so what's the problem?

P: Well – the things. Those gifts. Where do I start? OK, take the ring, for instance.

E: That was a wonderful ring, wasn't it?

P: It might have been, but – I never saw it. Look – you do actually realise, don't you, that you mimed putting that ring on my finger? There was no ring.

E: The cloak—

P: No, stop. There was no cloak. There were no sandals. There was no ring. You mimed them all. You know you did. That calf. That fatted calf is still running around fatted and fit as a fiddle in the pen outside. I cannot believe I sat around with everyone else pretending to eat veal. It was all mimed. There was actually nothing there!

E: Ah, yes, but they were symbols – powerful symbols.

P: Symbols are fine, but you can't protect your feet with symbols. You can't get a square meal from symbols. I don't feel forgiven. I haven't met the Father.

E: (*intensely*) Look, let me explain. You have met him – through us. You meet him and receive forgiveness through our togetherness, our fellowship. At our meetings. We all do.

P: I don't. Look – I have to confess I quite enjoyed all the mimes and rhymes and special times for a while, but not any more. I want to meet my Father. I want to be forgiven. I want it to be real.

E: OK, you know what – I've got a book here about the true nature of faith that's helped thousands of people. I think it will really speak into your problem. It's by someone who's been through all the same—

P: I don't want anyone or anything else to speak into my problem, thank you very much. There's only one thing I want. The thing I've wanted from the beginning. I want to go home.

The Armour of God

There are themes that Bridget and I return to again and again when we lead events at Scargill. One of these is Paul's famous 'Armour of God' metaphor. Like the Parable of the Prodigal Son, you can squeeze it forever. There will always be another drop of something interesting. The belt of truth and the helmet of salvation get a mention here.

Paul did so enjoy his metaphors, didn't he? I understand that completely, given my personal temptation to extend a beloved pet conceit beyond the point where it continues to be useful. This is what Paul (if it was Paul) actually says:

> *Therefore put on the full armour of God, so that when the day of evil comes, you may be able to stand your ground, and after you have done everything, to stand. Stand firm then, with the belt of truth buckled round your waist, with the breastplate of righteousness in place, and with your feet fitted with the readiness that comes from the gospel of peace. In addition to all this, take up the shield of faith, with which you can*

> *extinguish all the flaming arrows of the evil one. Take*
> *the helmet of salvation and the sword of the Spirit,*
> *which is the word of God.*
>
> (Eph. 6:13–17)

Some years ago I made the flippant, but fairly accurate, point that my store of available clothing did not include many of these items. In my spiritual wardrobe I discovered the Y-fronts of weariness, the knickers of non-involvement, the long johns of lust, the drainpipe trousers of doubt, a pink plastic sword borrowed from a very small friend of mine and the balaclava of bewilderment. I think things have improved a little since then, but I never have been able to bring myself to actually throw away that balaclava.

Perhaps there are times when it becomes necessary to actually take off the armour of God, because it can become uncomfortably heavy and start to hurt. Someone we know, on reaching a point of profound weariness and disillusionment, was commanded to 'Get straight up those stairs to your room, my girl, and put on the armour of God!' A cup of tea and a friendly arm round the shoulders might have been a great deal more useful on that particular occasion. The application of these metaphorical principles in real life needs to be considered carefully and in direct relation to the person or situation that we are facing. The armour of God can really pinch sometimes.

Coming from a rather different direction, a young shepherd called David, faced with the prospect of battling Goliath in the Old Testament, would have known exactly what I am talking about. For this task, the king's ponderously heavy armour was an alien hindrance. He needed just two things. One was a weapon he knew he could use well. That was his sling. The other was a friend at his side who could be trusted. That was God. As we all know, it worked. Next time the armour might come in handy. Maybe. Maybe not.

Having said all that, of course there are interesting and useful things to be learned from Paul's list of military accoutrements.

A small observation about the 'belt of truth'. It strikes me that a significant and familiar observation can be offered in this connection. If you don't put your belt of truth on and tighten it properly, your trousers are likely to fall down. Embarrassment, ignominy and a sad sense of failure may follow. It happens to many in the church. It has happened to me. I am sure others would have a far more profound point to make on the same subject, but this will do to be going on with. And I should add that the same point applies equally to braces, however colourful.

What next? Well, what about the helmet of salvation?

What does a helmet do? It protects your head and, presumably, the things inside your head. Your brain, thoughts, feelings, motivation, metaphorical heart – all those things. Where does salvation fit into that?

Sitting back and thinking about this question reminds me of times in the past when things have looked pretty hopeless. There was a particular period in my life when all I could hang on to was the love of family, and a few friends who were powered more by love than religion. Sometimes I would take one of my small children onto my lap and draw warmth and safety from the knowledge that, at this moment, on this day, at a time when that child could not possibly understand what I was going through, my head and heart and hope survived because of their love.

The thief dying by inches on his cross next to Jesus had a much more unexpected, last-minute experience of the same kind of thing. Suddenly, at a time when failure and pain and death must have been displacing everything else in his head, he saw, in the eyes of the man beside him, the barely believable possibility of happy ever after.

'Please remember me when you get there.'

'No problem. I'll see you later.'

Perhaps we need to rescue and resurrect the promise of happy ever after, a fairy-tale concept if ever there was one. This prospect, unless we have been grossly misinformed, lies at the very heart of everything that God is trying to do in this world. Yet there is a risk that we abandon the sweetness of this magical promise, perhaps because of a fear that we will confuse the real and the fantastical in a childish way and – horror of horrors! – even use the wrong language. We can and should sometimes enjoy a sense of true romance in the journeying that we have done with Jesus. Not the romance that happens between human beings, wonderful as that can be, but the romance of joy and despair and tough struggle and deep puzzlement and sudden revelation and the recurring flood of light and hope when darkness seems impenetrable.

That hope, that divine assurance that living happily ever after really is on the cards, is the helmet that protects and holds my head together. Now and then I forget how important it is.

Moaning

Before Scargill reopened, a group of us spent a few very enjoyable days at a Christian hotel, taking some time to pray about what might form the core of a set of promises

*to be made by new Community members. Not an easy task.
Everyone had ideas, but we shared a desire that folk should
not be asked to promise the impossible. That evening at
supper we were struck by the unusual cheerfulness of the
lady who served us, especially as we had seen her working
incredibly hard all day.*

*Explaining that we were in the process of forming a new
community, we asked what she considered an important
item to include in the promises.*

*'Keep the moaning inside until the right moment to let it
out,' was her rather surprising reply.*

That little nugget of wisdom found its way into the original
promises we settled on, and turned out to be a very valuable
daily reminder of the lifesaving need to occasionally vent
frustrations to the right person at the right time – and also
of the negative impact of continual moaning at the wrong
time.

A memory springs to mind. It concerns someone I once
knew, now busily engaged in cheering up the drooping
inhabitants of a part of the world very far away from here.
I shall call him Fred.

Fred had developed a most annoying habit. During group
debates or discussions, he would ask the rest of us a question, tell us how we were going to answer it, and then tell us
we were wrong. You want an example? Here is one.

'What do all of you think is the fundamental problem
with our church?' Flat, ham of a hand upraised to prevent
replies. 'Yes, I know you're going to say it's something to do
with outreach, but it's not. It's something else. I'll tell you
the main thing that's wrong with our church . . .'

Fred's wearily hectoring tone, and his automatic exclusion of us brain-dead ones from the discussion, became seriously infuriating. We tried hard to be Christian about it. Patience, forgiveness, grace – we exuded all that sort of stuff. Eventually, however, it became an unstated but indisputable fact that if something didn't change, we would probably have had to kill him – in love, that is. Fortunately, this less-than-spiritual solution to the problem was avoided by one of us, wiser and possibly more grounded than the rest of us, taking Fred aside and explaining, firmly but gently, that his habitual moaning dismissal of other people's opinions was unpleasant and unhelpful. Fred listened, and he did change – for most of the time.

We are very fortunate to have the example of Jesus. He could be very direct, shockingly so sometimes, but often when someone asked an important question – something like, 'Who is my neighbour?' – his reply came in the form of a story. Why? Well, we don't like being told off or moaned at. We don't listen. Why would we? It doesn't work. We love stories, though. Stories work well. They create space and opportunity for us to work out answers for ourselves, and those, as Jesus knew full well, are the answers we are much happier to own, and the ones that are more likely to last.

Moaning? It gets you nowhere.

So, Fred or Jesus? Jesus, I think.

Truth and Originality

One year at Scargill House, Bridget and I hosted our annual weekend for writers who are also Christians. It was all about writing short stories.

My own relatively brief input was a talk that included some thoughts on truth and originality in the context of creative arts, and it occurred to me that this subject might appeal to a wider audience and have a more general application.

You will not be at all surprised to learn that the most helpful comment I have heard or read on this theme springs from the fertile mind of C. S. Lewis. His contention was that originality in any form of artistic expression cannot be generated by either laborious or feverish attempts to invent something original. Rather, he maintains, if we approach our creative task with a determination to tell the truth, there is a far greater chance that we will automatically produce work that is truly new and original.

This simple argument has been of enormous help to me, but I have realised that we do have to ask ourselves what it actually means. A plain statement of what we believe to be true is clearly not guaranteed to be creative in terms of what that word is usually taken to mean. We have often quoted this little rhyme:

> It was 1983 when I asked Jesus into my life,
> Closely followed, three days later, by my wife.

True and stolidly worthy as this statement might be, it is hard to see how anyone might regard it as an example of creativity. Or imagine a gathering of Christians in which the contributions are as follows:

Weekly meeting of a housegroup attached to Saint Michael and All Angles – the church of plain truth

LEADER: Vernon, would you like to start?

VERNON: (*nervously and slowly, but with the muted excitement of one who, despite his humility, has been granted a revelation*) Er, yes. I'd just like to say that I now know something I didn't know before. It's about distance. (*pause for effect*) The distance from Croydon to Littlehampton is exactly fifty-six and a half miles, and it takes one hour and twenty minutes to do the drive on a good day – probably more on a Friday during rush hour.

Much solemn nodding and muttered thankings (more than one thanking) of the Lord.

LEADER: (*awestruck by the profundity*) Vernon, thank you so much! Right. Grant, are you happy to share?'

GRANT: Oh, OK. (*clears throat as he prepares to release his bombshell*) I'd like to just say that fracking has created a shale gas boom in the United States.

Confused reaction as some raise their arms and thank the Lord, and others look a bit puzzled and don't.

LEADER: (*solemnly and reflectively*) A shale gas boom. Well! (*looks around the group*) Wow, everybody. Janine (*jovially and with a playful punch in the air*) – hit us with some truth.

JANINE: (*she's been waiting, visibly filled with contained exultation*) So, just this morning, in my quiet time, I learned something completely new. If you – and this is what I did – if you divide 3,764,196 by nine, it comes to exactly – exactly 418,244!

ALL: Hallelujah! Oh, yes! Praise his name! Jesus indeed said that he came to divide . . . (*etc.*)

LEADER: (*almost tearful with joy*) Leonora, we've had three amazing contributions. Do you want to go fourth and multiply . . .?

Child of the Devil

One of our many teaching weeks at Scargill was entitled 'Where there's a well there's a way'. As the brighter ones among you will immediately guess, the subject of water was a dominant feature of those five days, not least because of a sky that wept like a repentant sinner until the final morning, when sunshine flashed and the most violently vivid rainbow we had ever witnessed seemed to speak passionately to us through one of the big windows that look out onto the valley. I suspect that everyone who saw that rainbow owned it in their own way as a sign of peace.

Sometimes, though, the rainbow effect has to reach back a long way into a person's life before genuine peace is possible.

There is an awful lot of water in the Bible. There are fascinating details about wells and cisterns and brooks and rivers and lakes and seas. There is also a moment when Jesus announces that anyone who gives even a cup of cold water to the least of his disciples will be rewarded. At one point during the week, we thought about those words.

It is a wonderful cushion of a promise, but what if the gift has been poisoned by the giver? I recalled an actual incident from my distant past.

I had been booked to speak at a church in the far north of England. On that chilly autumn evening I was picked up outside a railway station by a lady called Janet. She was to be my driver for the evening. This is more or less how the conversation went:

J: Hello, Adrian. I'm Janet. I'm taking you to the church and I'll be running you back to the station afterwards.

A: Ah, brilliant. Thanks for taking the job on, I really appreciate it. Nice, warm, comfortable car, too.

J: No problem. I wanted to do it. I volunteered, actually.

A: Oh – that's nice. Thanks very much.

J: (*after a pause*) You probably don't remember it, but we've met before.

A: Really? Recently, do you mean?

J: No, it was three or four years ago. You came to speak at my church – well, the church I used to go to just on the border. In Duncalk. A few miles from here.

A: (*struggling*) Duncalk . . .

J: Duncalk Baptist. The pastor was called Alec Downs.

A: (*relieved*) Of course! Got it! Actually, I spoke there a couple of times. Got on really well with Alec. A good man.

J: (*something less than agreement*) Mm.

A: (*thoughtful pause*) So – you left there?

J: Had to.

A: You had to? Good heavens. Why?

J: Because of Alec. (*grim pause*) What he said to me.

A: What he said to you? What did he say?

J: (*deep breath*) I find this hard to say, but – well, Alec told me that I was a child of the devil.

A: A child of the devil?

J: That's what he said. He called me a child of the devil. So I left. I had to.

A: I see. Hmm . . .

Conversation lapsed after that. I remembered Alec well. I'd really liked him, and I was finding it almost impossible to imagine him saying something like that. It just didn't seem to fit.

Later, after the event, on the way back to the station, I asked Janet a question:

A: Janet, you know what you said when you picked me up earlier – about what Alec said to you?

J: Yes?

A: If you don't mind – just tell me again what he said.

J: He called me a child of the devil. That's why I left.

A: A child of the devil.

J: That's right.

A: So he used those actual words, did he? He said, 'Janet, you are a child of the devil.'

J: Yes.

A: Those exact, precise words. 'You are a child of the devil.'

J: (*a sudden, oddly shocked, uncomfortable adjustment*) Well – he said that my behaviour wasn't what he would expect from a child of God. So – obviously, he was calling me a child of the devil, wasn't he?

A: Aaah! I see . . .

The rest of the journey was not comfortable. Over the previous two or three years, how many other people had heard Janet's version of her reason for leaving Duncalk Baptist Church? How many had repeated the story? How much darker and deeper had the lie become as it spread? Perhaps the most disturbing thing was that, until I pushed her a bit, Janet seemed to have ended up convincing even herself that Alec really had used those words.

It can easily happen when we get hurt. I know the process all too well. We sort through a selection of possible responses to the person who has made us feel so angry and wretched. At least one of those responses is likely to be some kind of fake forgiveness, designed to hurt and to take obscure revenge rather than to help and heal. Another might be a defensive distortion of the facts when we describe our grievance to others. That was Janet's refuge.

I have wrestled with these temptations myself. They can burn in us.

I'm afraid the right answer is usually sacrificial. You were afraid I was going to say that, weren't you? In the end, all we can do is sit as quietly as we can with our discarded weapons surrendered on the floor in front of us and ask God if he will be kind enough to let us know the mind of Christ and help us to proceed accordingly. It quite often works.

A cup of living water is always pure, and it can work wonders. But like some sort of spiritual Novichok, a tiny drop of poisoned truth can cause an awful lot of harm.

Hidden in Plain View

We have always really enjoyed exploring the Bible with guests, especially when we are able to shine a new light on passages that have become so familiar that we hardly notice them. The conference entitled 'Hidden in Plain View' was one of many occasions when we set ourselves the task, as modern-day disciples, of following the desire of Jesus that we open our minds.

It was even a little alarming to hear Jesus say that the Spirit blows where it pleases. Here is the full quote from John 3:8:

> *The wind blows wherever it pleases. You hear its*
> *sound, but you cannot tell where it comes from or*
> *where it is going. So it is with everyone born of the*
> *Spirit.*

If we look honestly at the Gospels, and equally honestly at our own response to what is written, we may, if we submit to being blown in unexpected directions by the Spirit, be challenged to accept that 1 Corinthians 13:12 is absolutely, and perhaps reassuringly accurate:

> *For now we see through a glass, darkly; but then face*
> *to face: now I know in part; but then shall I know even*
> *as also I am known.*
>
> (1 Cor. 13:12, KJV)

When we return to things or people or places that we once knew well, they can seem bigger or smaller, more colourful or surprisingly dull. Two reasons, perhaps.

First, the thing or persons or places are not themselves the real point. The important thing is what happened in or to us when we were in close contact with them. Falling in love, for instance, can convert the dullest of environments into a fairyland.

Second, and similarly, our interpretation of the past or the collected fragments of a recollection crystallise over time into something that we perceive as an accurate picture of the way things were. Discovering the flaws in such a picture can be bewildering or even very hurtful.

For me, the Enid Blyton 'Adventure' series is a clear example of memory being sabotaged by fact. I loved those books.

Island of Adventure. Valley of Adventure. Circus of Adventure. When I was a boy, they were real, solid, filled with colour and fascination. The characters – Lucy-Ann, Jack, Philip, Dinah and even Kiki the parrot – were genuine, rounded characters, people I loved so much. I wanted to know them. I wanted to be with them. I would have stepped into their world, if the back of my particular wardrobe had been a little more versatile.

Reading them once more as a young teenager was profoundly puzzling. A bit hurtful, and something of a shock. It was as though vast areas of this world I remembered had been scrubbed or thrown away, leaving something quite shallow and lacking in sparkle and depth and attraction. It was – dull.

So, what had happened? Had it been genius or luck on Enid Blyton's part? She certainly created spaces, but it was obviously me who filled them in. I furnished, decorated, adorned them with everything that was needed. Each time I read a new 'Adventure' book, I wasn't so much reading a book by an author as entering joyfully into a world that I loved. There was no critique. It was real.

Interesting that growing up, and thirty-four years of writing myself, has made it difficult – not impossible, but difficult – to experience that belief and wholehearted involvement in the same way when I read fiction.

So can something a bit similar to that process of realisation happen with the Bible, and the New Testament in particular? It is possible to absorb commonly held views about the four Gospels that might not survive careful examination. Sometimes, of course, this can be as simple as the fact that I haven't got round to properly reading the relevant passages for myself. I recall, for instance, the shock of realising that most of the highly significant Bethany story consists of a mere handful of verses. So very much in such a small container.

Does God reward good behaviour and obedience? If your answer is a typically dismal negative, it might be worth taking another look at the sixth chapter of Matthew, but beware the twist in the teaching.

On a lighter note, did Jesus tell people to go and talk to a fox? Some will know immediately what that's all about.

Does Jesus make two statements in the Gospels that he knows to be untrue? (I'll leave that for you to work out for yourself.)

Perhaps we need to throw open a few windows.

Are you aware that there was an occasion when the crowds that came to see Jesus were so great that people trampled each other? Concordance time.

So, given the fact that our view may need to be adjusted, where does this leave us? I can only answer for myself. My enjoyment and profound appreciation of the Bible has not diminished as a consequence of discovering that some of my memories of Scripture are faulty or distorted. My excitingly vivid Enid Blyton world certainly did not survive, but more concentrated and contextual study of Scripture over the last few decades has brought an enrichment and relevance that I could never have anticipated as a younger man. I am quite sure that people like Richard Wurmbrand, and Dietrich Bonhoeffer, and countless millions of others who saw darkly and only in part just like us, have preferred prison or torture or death, or being laughed at, or giving up a person or a life that they loved, because they also knew the strange quality of words that can sometimes have a surprisingly active life of their own. I suspect that the platform on which all these sufferers and martyrs stood was informed by biblical truth, and their feet must have been filled with truth. People vote with their feet, whatever anyone else says.

Having said all that, it seems to me very necessary that we learn to embrace the cloudy reflection in that glass and the half-formed knowledge that Paul talks about in his first letter to the Corinthians. C. S. Lewis, in his apologetic writings (apologetics, by the way, means defence of faith), produced arguments about the Christian faith that were very helpful to many people, but it was his children's literature that most successfully and profoundly conveyed the heart of his belief in Jesus. In the last part of his life, he was expressing thoughts that Mother Teresa would have fully understood, having suffered from depression and a sense of separation from God for much of her adult life. Here is a quote by Lewis from A. N. Wilson's biography:

> *If we cannot 'practise the presence of God', it is something to be able to practise the absence of God, to become increasingly aware of our unawareness till we feel like a man who should stand beside a great cataract and hear no noise, or like a man in a story who looks in a mirror and finds no face there, or a man in a dream who stretches out his hand to visible objects and gets no sensation of touch.*[3]

C. S. Lewis certainly knew and valued his Bible, but he had already begun to glimpse the incomprehensibility of the

---

[3] A. N. Wilson, *C. S. Lewis: A Biography* (London: HarperCollins, 1990).

person of God, and the challenge of maintaining and expressing his faith in that God without the need for a logical argument.

I must confess that there are times when I weary of theoretical Christianity. Let's be honest. Some things might be hidden or inexplicable, but others are in perfectly plain view, and might even reward some careful reflection. Here is an example from the Old Testament book of Micah.

> He has shown you, O mortal, what is good.
> And what does the LORD require of you?
> To act justly and to love mercy
> and to walk humbly with your God.

(Mic. 6:8)

Nobody claims that these biblical guidelines will be easy to follow, not least the present and future communities at Scargill, but they are plain and comprehensible and comfortable enough for most of us to at least have a go.

6

Matters of Life and Death
in Pandemic Times

I am writing these words in the spring of 2021, in the midst of the Covid pandemic that has had such a huge impact worldwide. In the United Kingdom, more than a hundred thousand people have died as a result of coronavirus. The number is still rising, but vaccines are now available and have been given to millions of people since December. Bridget and I recently had our first jab. There is some brightness in the air. Springtime is performing its slow surge, and we reach out to that powerful natural metaphor more than ever before. We would like to be positive, but a hope-famine has spread throughout the world. It is caused not by lack of faith, but by experience. By the time you read this, anything might have happened – or not happened.

This section of the book is born out of more than a year of suffering, heroism, hope, disappointment and unprecedented restrictions on our daily lives, at least in the West. I hope and pray that by the time you read this, all – or as much as possible – will be well.

Thoughts Amid the First UK Lockdown

I have enormously enjoyed writing letters for my website over the last few years. I suppose much of the enjoyment comes from the fact that, broadly speaking, I am free to say anything I want in the way that I choose. The letter that follows was a first reaction to the onset of the virus, and to our growing awareness that we were facing something darker and more lethal than anyone could have imagined. (Had you realised, by the way, that coronavirus is an anagram of 'carnivorous'?)

Dear anyone who reads this and everyone who doesn't,

The first thing to say about the coronavirus is that it's a &%^&£%&, $&%$&%, &*^%$^&, *^$% addition to all the other things that my family, most of those we know and many, many folks who contact us are already dealing with. Where is God in it? You would have to ask him.

I tell myself that if I were God I would not have let it happen. However, despite and because of a number of strange but convincing experiences, I am committed to trusting him both in darkness and in light. What is there to say? You will not be surprised to hear that three things occur to me and to my wife Bridget – we were steeped in Anglicanism for many years.

The first is one of the more common but less noticed attributes of love. Bridget and I have always been amazed by the elasticity and unlimited expanding properties of the human capacity for caring. Love can spread exactly as far as it needs to go, however far that turns out to be. This horrible virus is frightening a lot of people, but we are doing our best to remember and draw some hope from the knowledge that all of us, of any faith or none, can still be agents for the spreading of what might be described as a positive virus. The virus of love is powerful beyond belief.

It can cover a house or a street or a village or a town or a city or, potentially, the entire world. Superficial? No, there is nothing deeper or more practical in its effects than love.

The second thought is about scaffolding – no, don't drift off, it's worth hearing. Over the last ten years, Bridget and I have known what it means to face dismay and disappointment when bad times come, and the edifice of our faith begins to crack and fall apart under the pressure. We are certainly not alone in this experience. It is as though we have relied on scaffolding that, until now, has held us upright and apparently intact. The poles of this supporting structure can take many forms, including music, religious observance, Bible study, styles of prayer, upbringing or the company of like-minded others. These and a host of other poles and planks that are harmless or even valuable in themselves can, it seems, under the dark pressure of something as overwhelming as this ghastly coronavirus, suddenly fall away and fail to support the house of truth and love we had hoped was at the very centre of who we are.

Perhaps it is possible for this to be an unusually dramatic opportunity to reassess priorities. (If you are making snorting noises in response to this, I don't blame you. Snort as much as you like. It's still true.)

The third point is about stockpiling. There's been some fierce stuff going on. Houses stuffed with toilet rolls and bottles of antiseptic handwash. Queues of people like us in the seventy-plus bracket outside the supermarket first thing in the morning, made up of many people who are nice, and a few people who are certainly not. What is needed here is decidedly an attitude of mind, a determinedly generous perspective that allows the flowering of generosity and refuses to countenance the growth of a mean spirit.

Yes, it's obvious. Yes, it needs to happen.

The Israelites in the desert were not allowed or able to do any stockpiling. Manna fell from heaven and it was good stuff for twenty-four hours. After that it went off big-time – there was no point at all in packing snacks for the journey. The whole crowd complained loudly to Moses, but the lesson had to be learned. You get as much as you need for the time when you need it. Take it. Be thankful.

Those are our three feeble thoughts. I don't suppose they will change much, but if they offer glimmers of light in the present darkness, let us pray it will be enough.

Much love to those we know, and to those we don't,
Adrian

Days of Our Lives

From the beginning of April 2020, Bridget and I recorded sixty-three daily podcasts, under the title 'No Shore In Sight'. You can find them on YouTube. We did make some serious points in the course of those nine weeks, but we enjoyed many light moments as well, and the response from listeners made it very clear that a chance, an excuse, a reason to laugh was welcome and necessary. Our typical quirkiness helped as well.

When I resurrected something I had written in my mid-sixties about the way I viewed each day of the week, and particularly which colour and character I attributed to each, the response was overwhelming. Never mind global issues. Everyone had a view on the colour of Wednesday and Friday, and especially Sunday. We were quite surprised.

At the time in my life when I wrote this, I had been alive for sixty-six years, five months and one day, which adds up to 24,241 days altogether. Or to put it another way, I had enjoyed (or sometimes not enjoyed) 3,463 weeks. This means that I had experienced each day of the week on 3,463 occasions, including the day on which I wrote it, which was a Monday.

In all that time, as you can perhaps imagine, I had acquired some pretty strong views about all seven of the days, and I find that those views have not changed. Yours may be different, but that doesn't matter. These are mine.

Monday is as grey and as flat as slate for most people. Even when it isn't raining, it might as well be. Even when the sun shines, it rains. Even when there's a drought, it rains. Even when it's as dry as the driest thing in the history of the world – guess what? Yes, it rains.

Not on me, it doesn't. I work at home. Here, in my study, Monday is as charmingly blue as a hedge sparrow's egg. I like it, and it likes me. I stay dry. Even when it rains I enjoy watching it from my comfortable, dry place. So, have a good day at work. Don't get too wet.

Tuesday is sort of plump and squishy. A jelly-filled day that gets pushed into all sorts of shapes by people who suddenly realise that there are things left over from last Friday that should have been sorted out on Monday but weren't because they couldn't be bothered when they were putting up with all that rain. Tuesday is green. Not a bright, happy green, but maybe a shade less grim than the colour of mushy peas. I like mushy peas, by the way.

Wednesday is brown, like a creosoted fence. It is a rather grown-up day with a flat, stern, wooden, DIY sort of voice that tells you to get something practical done for heaven's sake, before the whole week becomes a waste of time. Sometimes, unexpectedly, Wednesday evening dresses up and dances around a bit, but only if you happen to have achieved a thing during the day. Between you and me, Wednesday is a bit up itself.

Thursday is a strange day. A unicorn of a day. Colour? Grey. Silvery grey. More exquisitely fine chain mail than heavy metal. Some gauze somewhere. What is gauze? Thursday is a woman, I think. She wafts and waves and beckons us on to the glittering path that will eventually take us to Friday.

Anything could happen on a Thursday, but it tends not to.

Friday. Ah, Friday! Friday is a sizzling, fish-filled, crackling fire of a day, a good time to go to the nearest fish and chip restaurant after work and have a Jumbo Haddock and chips with Tuesday-coloured peas and bread and butter and a pot of tea. Aaah!

(I would love to know someone called Jumbo Haddock. A large, gilled man with glassy eyes who doesn't believe in Cod.

'Hello, Jumbo,' I'd say. 'How are you, and Mrs Haddock, and all the little sprats?')

Friday is the colour of embers in a hot fire. It wakes me up into realising that Wednesday can shout as loudly as it wishes from two days ago, but it won't make any difference, because Friday is whispering and buzzing in my ear, 'Don't you worry, the weekend is almost here . . .'

You learn over the years that Friday evening is very often the best part of Saturday.

Saturday is yellow, almost golden, but not quite. The sandy beaches of Saturday are very alluring. A stroll in search of exotic shells. You almost never find them, but you might. Saturday plays a gentle tune of encouragement, but it also comes up with some jagged chords of challenge. Oh, Saturday, my old friend, such tender hopes I have placed in you over the years. Sometimes I have not been disappointed. A question I have always wanted to ask. Why, oh why, do you hang around with Sunday?

Sunday is a storm. Sometimes a dull storm, like unhappiness that never quite manages to cry, sometimes black skies with sudden amazing flashes of white light. Sunday has an identity crisis, perhaps because of being squashed between Saturday and Monday.

'I think I could have been a Saturday,' says Sunday in a sad, quiet voice. 'Actually, I think I was once. I can't quite remember. Never mind. Oh, and just for the record, I categorically refuse to accept responsibility for Monday.'

Sunday is either God's day off or humankind's day off. One or the other. Or both. No wonder it's confused. Poor day.

Goodbye. And have a good day.

A Fear of Tomatoes

During the course of the pandemic there has been a great deal said about fear. 'Faith, not fear' was and is the encouraging cry from some churches, and of course it makes sense, if you can manage it. The problem with fear is that there are so many things to be frightened of. I wrote a book called The Unlocking *once. It was supposed to be about tackling fear. I thought it would be mainly about other people's fears. In fact, I discovered a bewildering variety and number of fears in myself.*

In one of our early recordings during the initial lockdown we invited listeners to share their fears, including the more extreme ones. We heard from someone who has always had an irrational fear of water towers and were cheered to learn that this is actually classified as 'thalassophobia'. I kid you not.

Then, of course, it was our turn. Bridget confessed to such a panicky dread of making and taking telephone calls that she would sometimes rather throw the phone across the room to me than answer it herself.

Me? I had to admit that one of my irrational fears concerned fruit, and one type of fruit above all.

I have a longstanding problem with tomatoes.

There, I've said it. What a relief. I thought I never would.

The tomato issue is complex and multifaceted. I have used tomato ketchup for as long as I can remember; in fact, one of my favourite rhyming couplets as a child was this one:

Shake, oh shake the ketchup bottle,
First none'll come, and then a lot'll.[4]

The thing you have to understand, though, is that my innocent, childish mind never made the connection between actual tomatoes and the ketchup that was made from them. Tomatoes were tomatoes. Ketchup was ketchup.

Life was so much simpler then. As a matter of interest (and I know you are riveted with interest), it wouldn't have mattered in those early days if I *had* seen the connection. The tomatoes

---

[4] Richard Armour (1906–89).

grown in our greenhouse were sweet, good-natured little creatures with a distinct tomato flavour. I loved them. And yes, I
ate them. As I vaguely recall Oscar Wilde putting it:

Yet each man eats the fruit he loves.[5]

As the years passed, my liking for ketchup continued, but a
pall of darkness slowly came to envelop my relationship with
tomatoes themselves. Those gentle, balmy, far-off greenhouse days were gone forever, and the things that continued
to brazenly masquerade as tomatoes were not as in former
times. They were sour. They were either gruesomely squishy
or jeeringly resistant to the penetration of human teeth.
Some were ludicrously big. Giant scarlet packages of bland-
ness. They tasted of nothing yet seemed mindlessly unaware
of their own deficiencies. Moreover, they refused to mix
freely with the rest of the salad – too proud, one suspects, to
be associated with the colour green. There is surely no uglier
manifestation of racism than salad discrimination.

I became an abstainer, and I remain so to this day (other
than in cheese and tomato sandwiches, which I really like;
and ketchup, as I've already mentioned; and sliced, uncooked
tomatoes on toast with a dribble of oil and some bits of
basil. Also tomato soup, my favourite soup of all; and
tomato relish which is good for dipping – oh, and I nearly
forgot, sundried tomatoes are delicious with olives).

Those who do not yet share my belief in God might be
interested to know that, since finishing the previous

---

[5] Oscar Wilde (1854–1900), 'Yet Each Man Kills the Thing He Loves', from
Selected Poems of Oscar Wilde.

paragraph, I have spoken on the phone to my friend Peter Ryder, who, on hearing that I was writing about tomatoes, told me the story of his own Damascus Road experience in this context. Peter's revelation did not happen precisely on the Damascus Road. It was on the road to Pocklington, a small market town at the foot of the Yorkshire Wolds, but the effect was similar.

Peter stopped in a layby to eat a sandwich that had been prepared for him by his wife. As he bit into it, he entered into what he describes as a dual reality. He found himself eating pieces of tomato, a fruit or vegetable that hitherto had been anathema to him. At the same instant he realised that he was not only eating but also *enjoying* the food that he had vowed would never pass his lips again.

Life was never the same after that. Peter stopped kicking against the goads and gave himself over to tomatoes, especially in the south of France. Now I ask you, was that God, or was that God?

If I am being truly honest, there are scars from wounds caused by betrayal and disappointment experienced in orange, satsuma and tangerine contexts.

This is largely my wife's fault, I am sad to say. We have been married for many, many years, and an otherwise happy relationship has been soured only by her inexplicable determination to feed me oranges, satsumas and tangerines that are simply not sweet enough to eat. I end up believing her seductive lies every time – every single time.

'Come on, just have a little bit of this orange. You'll love it. It's really juicy and sweet.'

'That's what you said the last time, and it wasn't. It was sour and I hated it.'

'Yes, but this one's different. I tell you – this one's almost *too* sweet for me to eat.'

'No, I don't think I'll—'

'Oh, go on, just one little teensy-weensy segment. Just pop it in your mouth.'

'Oh, all right, go on then . . .'

'Tell me what you think.'

'Aargh!'

Inedible, as usual. Had to spit it out, as usual. Betrayed and misled, as usual. Mind you, I shouldn't be surprised. This is a woman who eats grapefruit halves for pleasure. Without sugar! (I only learned about this unfortunate predilection after we had recited our vows before God and the vicar. Grounds for annulment, some might say.) She made all those promises, but never thought to mention that a variety of citrus fruits would ever stand between us.

Ah well, we have had it out, and there are compensations. My wife and I are agreed on one thing. He is the vine and we are the branches. And any branch that does not bear fruit gets cut off and burned. So we have agreed that Bridget will do whatever is the spiritual equivalent of tomatoes, oranges and all other citrus fruits, and I'll do bananas, ripe pears, strawberries and other sweet, unaggressive items. So far, it seems to be working.

Patience in Lockdown

This piece originally appeared in an edition of The Plough[6], *a magazine published by the Bruderhof Community.*

---

[6]   Autumn 2020 edition of *Plough Quartley*.

Readers' reactions to this tale of a life endured in the constrictions of lockdown interested me greatly. Some seemed to understand from it exactly what I thought I had been trying to say. Others arrived at an almost opposite interpretation. I make no judgement on those differing responses, but I do recall reading somewhere an assertion that books and stories read us just as much as we read them. I thought these words a little trite at the time, but perhaps, now I think about it, this is bound to be true.

What do you think this story is about?

Dear Mary,

Something has happened. But who can I tell? Everything in me wanted to ring and ask you to come round. Would have been a waste of time, of course. You never came back from Exeter. Stranded in your sister's house since the lockdown began. I have no address and no telephone number.

Oh, Mary, I have missed our Wednesday mornings. We always had stories to share about the lessons God was teaching us, and I particularly enjoyed working out the meaning of the pictures that the Holy Spirit gave us for each other. And the coffee and cake, of course. Always Battenberg at yours, coffee and walnut at mine.

In those two hours God seemed to really exist, didn't he? I never told you this, Mary, probably because I was embarrassed, but quite often, after you went, it felt as if God had gone home with you and left me on my own. I cried sometimes. How silly. God is everywhere. I know that. He never leaves us.

Surely.

During this strange time the phone does ring from time to time, but it has never been you. I know we are supposed to give our whole lives to God to decide what should happen, and I did pray for peace of mind and forgiveness for my lack of trust, but I cannot stop wondering why you never call me. Of course, I hope you have not got this horrible virus, and even if you have stayed well, you may have just been too busy to get in touch. Perhaps you had to concentrate hard on looking after your poorly sister during the lockdown. I do understand. She is your priority. You have to decide what is the most important thing and then do it.

The trouble is that since God gave me that very clear picture, the one that finally made us decide to leave our Bible study group, there really is nobody else to hear my news. What would happen if I went back and presented myself to Mr You-know-who? Imagine me sitting in that oh-so-calm room of his, full of straight lines and bookcases, my face all flushed as I try to explain what has happened and working like mad to stop the excitement from bursting out all at once. I couldn't cope, Mary.

You know what I'm talking about. The little grown-up smile that makes me feel like a toddler. The way he leans back and pats the air with his hands to make me and my feelings slow down. That sensible, kind voice saying we have to test everything to make sure it really is from God. I forgive him and love him as we are told we must, but I trust and believe that the gift my heavenly Father has provided is too important for me to risk it being spoiled.

No, you are the only one who will understand, Mary, so I am writing this to you, and believing in faith that, despite everything, the Lord will provide a way for my letter to reach you. I want you to read it and write back to say what you think.

This is what happened to me.

Sorry, just one more thing to make clear before I tell you. I have said that I miss you very much, and I do. That is difficult enough, but the loneliness of these past weeks goes so deep that it hurts right inside my chest sometimes. Yes, you and I know that Christians have no need to be lonely. God is sufficient for all our needs. But that lovely American preacher on our last DVD did say that sometimes we are given a wilderness season, a gift from God that helps our faith to grow strong. I think I might be in one of those. I do my daily prayer and quiet time each morning, and I make sure I take the walk that we are allowed in the afternoon, but the rest of each day in my wilderness season has been longer and more difficult to fill than any other time in my life. You need to know that. But my faith will grow.

Surely.

This is what happened. One day, in a drawer I had been saving because it was the very last one left to tidy, I found an old pack of playing cards. I took them out to play a game of patience, or solitaire as it is sometimes called. I played it on that little gate-legged table of my mother's below the front window where we enjoy our coffee and cake on Wednesdays.

You and I are comfortable with confessing our sins to each other, Mary, so I can tell you this. I became totally absorbed, perhaps even a little obsessed, with this game. As you know, patience follows the same pattern with each separate play but varies in the way it works out because the cards are shuffled before each game and are in a new, random order. I seldom win, perhaps because I am always so strict about only going three times through the remaining pack after laying out the first seven rows.

I filled three days of my wilderness hours with endless games of patience. After that I began to feel guilty and distanced from God. Late on the third day I knelt in a wretched state at my bedside to confess this growing addiction and to ask the Lord for his help in overcoming temptation.

I began my quiet time the following morning in low spirits. As I reluctantly opened my Bible, I found myself sinking into a sort of deep swamp of unhappiness. The very thought of not being allowed to sit happily at my window and lay my cards out after finishing my quiet time and clearing away the breakfast things was almost more than I could bear.

This was the moment when the miracle happened.

The Bible verses accompanying my devotional notes came from the seventh chapter of Ecclesiastes. I could hardly believe my eyes. On this morning of all mornings, verse 8 of chapter 7 contained these exact words:

The end of a matter is better than its beginning,
and PATIENCE is better than pride.

I have put that word in capital letters, but I certainly did not search for those verses. No opening of the Bible at random. Nothing of that sort. The words were simply staring me in the face. I know you will understand the joy they brought. God was there. He was speaking to me. I was not alone. Hallelujah! I could almost hear an actual voice saying, 'Janice, you were right to be concerned about your absorption. But the end of this concern will be much better than the beginning. Your pride deceived you into the error of believing I could not be involved in the small things of your life. Let me presence myself in your games, and you will witness a mighty work.'

Oh, Mary! I had goosebumps as I sat down to begin my next round of patience. God would be with me, and I could barely wait to see how his will would be made manifest. I am bad at shuffling, but as I did my best to mix the cards thoroughly I reflected on the fact that their order would no longer be random. It would be ordained by God himself. A thrilling thought. What would he teach me?

Laying the cards out face down in seven rows, one in the first, and two, three, four, five, six and seven in each of the others, was almost, dare I say, a priestly experience. My hand trembled as I began to turn over the bottom card on each of the seven rows. I clearly recall the first six cards that were revealed. There was a seven of spades, a nine of diamonds, a four of diamonds, a two of hearts, a three of spades and a five of clubs. It was, for me, a hug of affirmation from God. Even before I turned the seventh card I knew with delicious anticipation that there were, at the very least, three moves possible before needing to take extra cards from the rest of the pack.

Then I turned the seventh card. I stared, unable to believe what met my eyes. Then, as I grasped the truth, my heart seemed to drop like a stone in my body.

Mary, that final card was a joker. A joker, Mary! I had forgotten to remove the jokers before shuffling my cards. I could see in human terms how that might happen, but what of the spiritual meaning? Where was God in this? Why had he given such clear guidance through Scripture? If he truly was in charge, surely he would not have allowed me to make such a foolish mistake.

Surely.

I held the card aloft, closed my eyes and prayed for wisdom and insight.

Moments passed. When the revelation came it was – oh, it was like a light being switched on, or bells suddenly ringing, or a letter from a friend plopping onto the mat beneath the front door. A joker. Of course! Mary, God was the joker. I had forgotten that our God has a sense of humour. You and I often say that, don't we? He delights to laugh with his children. That joker card, allowed by him to be placed in the very centre of my game, was a reminder that he laughs and smiles with me, even at the most unexpected moments.

With a grateful heart I collected my cards together, carefully removed the jokers, shuffled the pack as well as I was able and laid my seven rows out once more.

Mary, we have always tried to tell each other the truth. I am determined to do that now. The truth is, I really thought God might let me win that next game of patience, I suppose as a sort of reward or little present after teaching me the lesson about the joker. I wanted

him to be kind to me. I wanted to be special. Yes, I
know that sounds silly. I can't help it. It just felt such a
right and happy thing to happen.

At first I thought he was going to let me win. Some of
that next game was like one of those dreams where
things make sense at last and you know you are heading
for the place where you belong. It was amazing.

One after another, the four aces emerged from the
extra pack, or came into view as I turned a new card in
one of the rows. I was so uplifted, Mary. Red tens on
black jacks. Black nines on red tens. Sevens on eights.
Twos on threes. Jacks on queens. God and me and the
cards moving together in a perfect, swift, joyous way
that made success seem inevitable.

It was not to be.

A king appeared like a horrid full stop – the last thing
I wanted to see. It ended my game.

And yet, as you will have guessed, it was another, and
even more important, lesson to be learned. The presence of the King of heaven will always be the most
important thing in our lives. Human ideas of success
are as nothing compared to that wonderful truth.

So, there you are. That was my exciting thing, and of
course I am truly grateful for every bit of his affirmation and teaching. As long as the Lord controls the
cards that are dealt into our lives, we know that we can
never lose in the most important sense. With God, nothing is random. That has to be true, doesn't it?

Surely.

Oh, but Mary, I did so enjoy the middle part of that
game. A real – whoosh! It was like flying. Like all sorts

of things. And at least, in the end, it was the king of hearts.

I hope you will ring. I hope you get back from Exeter one day. I only ever have coffee and walnut cake when you come. I so look forward to giving you a hug.

With much love from your locked-down friend,
Janice xxxxxxx

PS, I meant to say: in the course of that game the Lord marvellously healed my obsession with patience. I hardly play at all now.

You Are Worth More Than Many Sparrows

There were at least two unexpectedly positive aspects of life in lockdown confinement. One was the way in which workers who had previously gone unnoticed were suddenly being publicly affirmed. These included, among others, workers in care homes for the elderly, refuse collectors and supermarket staff, all being seen and fully appreciated at last. It was at least a bit of a break from the understandable but tediously unremitting worship of glamour and fame.

Another bright spot was a general flaring of interest in gardening and the enjoyment of putting out food for birds, with reported sightings of a huge variety of garden birds. Gardening is not generally my scene, but we both became determined to research the various types of seeds and other foods that were bound to tempt said huge variety of birds into our back garden.

We bought and set out feeders and feed, dragged our very effective binoculars out from wherever they had ended up, and sat expectantly and excitedly on comfortable chairs in our back sitting room. We also armed ourselves with a book featuring coloured pictures of every garden bird in the United Kingdom, so that when huge varieties arrived we would immediately be able to flick through the pages and identify them.

This dramatised account of our first experience is almost unbearably close to the truth.

B: OK, well, all the stuff's out there. We've got fat balls and a wild seed mix on the left. That should bring all sorts of birds, especially in the winter.

A: Great. Right. What about the Nyjer seeds? It would be really nice to get some goldfinches coming down. I can't believe those birds. They're so pretty.

B: They're adorable. Oh, siskins like Nyjer seeds as well. Should get some of them.

A: Siskins are finches as well, aren't they? Big beaks.

B: That's right. What else? Oh, I put some flaked maize on the ground around the feeders as well. That's for the blackbirds. And I haven't forgotten the tits and the green-finches. Apparently they go mad for sunflower seeds.

A: Excellent. Lots of good old millet for the house sparrows and the collared doves. We're bound to get *some* sparrows, aren't we?

B: Why not? They've got to eat as well. I just hope the other birds don't – you know – crowd them out.

A: Yes, that would be sad, wouldn't it? Really unfair. Poor old sparrows. We'll keep an eye on that. Heh, wouldn't it be fantastic if we had a greater spotted woodpecker soon? Beautiful red on their heads. They do come into gardens sometimes. I can't wait. Do you want first go with the binoculars?

B: No, you go ahead. So exciting! I wonder what our very first bird will be.

A: OK, let's have a look. (*pause*) Erm, nothing yet. Wait a minute! There is one! There's one! Wow! Wow! Straight for the Nyjer seeds!

B: (*clapping hands*) Goldfinch?

A: N-n-n-no, it's more of a browny-coloured sort of bird, I think. Not quite sure . . .

B: Probably a siskin. Interesting. (*looks excitedly at book*). The question is – is it a European siskin or a Eurasian siskin? The Eurasian one's got a black head and a sort of—

A: Ha! No, no. I'm pretty sure it's a good old house sparrow.

B: I didn't think they were supposed to go for Nyjer seeds.

A: Well, this one does. Can't blame him. Grab a meal before the others get in.

B: (*pointing*) Wait a minute! There's another one! On the other feeder. Quick – give me the glasses. (*pause*) Now that's – that is – that is definitely – that is another sparrow. (*pause*) Oh, both the sparrows have flown away now. Wait a minute! (*excitedly*) A whole flock of birds – all over both feeders. Wow!

A: Fantastic! Now we're getting somewhere. What sort of birds?

B: Hold on – let me see. *Some* are sparrows, but . . . Ah! Ah!

A: What? What are the others?

B: You can look in a minute. (*pause*) I'm pretty sure the others are—

A: Tits?

B: N-n-no.

A: Reed buntings?

B: Definitely not reed buntings . . . Oh! They've all flown off at once.

A: Did you manage to work out what they were before they went?

B: Er, sparrows mostly – well, all sparrows. Oh! Look, look, look, look, look! One bird's come down all on his own. He must have frightened the others off. You look! You look! (*hands glasses over*) Come on! What is it?

A: Well, unless I'm very much mistaken, that is – come on, bird, turn round so that I can see your head. Ah! There we are. That is definitely – a sparrow. That one's cleared off as well now. (*lowers glasses*) I think that might be it for a while.

B: (*takes glasses*) You're probably right – just a minute! That is definitely *not* a sparrow!

A: Brilliant! What is it?

B: It's a pigeon. It's a great big, plump pigeon.

A: What's it doing?

B: (*slowly*) Not a lot. It's sitting in the water dish, reaching fatly up and pecking seed out of the food containers – like a drunk at a buffet. A great big, fat, stupid-looking pigeon. (*lowers glasses*) It's fallen off and flapped away.

A: (*a bit disappointed*) OK. Well, that seems to be it. So, what are you going to write on the first page of our new Ornithological Observation Log?

B: Millions of sparrows and one overweight pigeon, I suppose. (*she writes*)

A: Tell you what – bung a goldfinch in. Cheer us up a bit. No one'll know.

B: Well, for all we know one of those sparrows might have been a scruffy, elderly goldfinch.

A: Exactly! He'd be so flattered. Go on. Stick him down.

Treasures in Lockdown

Bridget and I found comfort and interest in identifying treasures that increased in value during that difficult period. There turned out to be more than we expected. Here are just a few, starting with Communion.

Communion has always meant a lot to me. C. S. Lewis talks about a sense of almost being physically touched by the connection that is made with Jesus when, at his earnest request, we put some oomph into remembering him. I agree, and I have come to believe that it probably does not really matter to God how bread and wine is shared in the technical sense. I have to confess, though, that generally speaking I have always preferred the Anglican way. Not, I hasten to add, because of anything to do with 'magic hands'. There are no hands magical or humble enough to qualify for the task in themselves. No, it is more piquant and dramatic than that, something to do with the journey that most of us have to make from seat to (Communion) rail, a journey that can be more safely and better taken with no excess baggage, though that is a tall order when we are hefting burdens that cannot easily be dumped under our chairs.

That row of backs, the varying sizes and shapes, the uncompromisingly equal distribution of what is available, both physically and spiritually. So sweet and strange. Impossible to read and understand in joined-up writing, and mysteriously unpredictable. Things can happen at the Communion table.

During lockdown, Bridget and I have been appreciating this act of remembering even more. On most Wednesday mornings we have enjoyed a Skype Communion with two close friends. In a rare moment of personal vulnerability, Jesus tells us how much he was longing for the event that we call the Last Supper. I think we have felt rather like that each Wednesday morning. We have been able to laugh a lot, cry a little, say ridiculous things, pray without feeling silly, stop to make a comment or change a line in the service we use, and enjoy the simple, staggering fact that the five of us are together in a magical mystery that punctuates the narrative of these dark times, and truly does lighten our darkness.

Communion is a treasure.

My treasure chest also contains a little chunk from the Old Testament. A friend who has long since gone off to do a bit of afterlife pioneering once showed me a verse in the book of Job, saying that he thought it might be something that could mean a lot to me as the years went by. I doubt he imagined this to be in any sense a spiritual revelation, but that is exactly what it was.

Chapter 29 in this great poem shows Job, beset by illness and confusion, remembering the time in his life when, as a truly authentic representative of God, he addressed the people and was very helpful to them. In the 24th verse, Job recalls, 'When I smiled at them, they scarcely believed it . . .'

A true and prophetic statement, indeed. Over the last three decades we have seen how many suffering believers respond with anything from mild surprise to total shock on learning that God might actually be constructively sympathetic in the midst of their devastation. He might even smile at them! They can scarcely believe it. God must be at least as nice as my mother invariably was, perhaps even a little nicer, if my now heavenly mansion-ensconced mother will excuse such heresy.

God's smile. Treasure.

One treasure seems to have increased in value. Permission to tell the truth. Now that is a strange thing for a Christian to bother to mention, do you not think? Of course we tell the truth. Surely.

Perhaps the problem is a fear that God will pop and disappear like a bubble if we poke him with any sharply pointed truth about how we actually feel. When I was a young Christian, I found it almost impossible to allow myself a clear expression of disappointment or failure or despair. I wanted God to be what he was supposed to be, and I was certainly not going to be the one who spoiled that by wilfully chucking my negative truth at him.

I understand my younger self. I sympathise. But it really is a load of old tosh, is it not? In terms of living the life of abundance that, as we all know, is a sort of strapline in the Gospel adverts, repressing the truth really is handicapping, to say the least.

We Christians respect the Psalms. We talk about how fortunate we are to have that implied permission to shout at the sky when all the tent pegs have come out and the tent is about to blow over the hedge into the river. Over the past six months, Bridget and I have heard from many, many people who simply cannot understand where God is or why such dark clouds seem to be enveloping them. Pronouncements from some Church sources say that we have nothing to fear, and of course there is a sort of ultimate truth contained within that statement, but in the meantime, down at ground level there is a lot to fear.

A modern psalm for many?

How are things at your end?
They're pretty rubbish down here.
(That's the edited version, by the way.)

Fortunately, if Job was right, and I suspect he was, God will be in the middle of our turmoil, not waiting disapprovingly on the sidelines for our attitudes to be improved.

The creator of the universe is used to it. Jesus told us that the truth will set us free, and it will. No need to be afraid of venting the pain. Jesus did it.

Permission to tell the truth. A treasure for these times.

One more treasure. The most important one. The onion in the stew. The struggler in the wilderness. The shepherd of the sheep. The forsaken victim. The man who never gave up. The resurrected one. My hero. Jesus.

A Creed for Now

Putting together a personal creed is an awkward business. As usual, that is because, by its very nature, truth imposes a tension between itself and the loyalty demanded by a loving relationship. Even as I write this sentence and say the words back to myself, I realise that it sounds like one of those statements that doesn't really mean anything when you take it to pieces.

I wish.

Passing through this extraordinary time, more and more Christians have found it difficult to work out what they do believe. I have found it helpful and interesting to construct a creed that reflects where I actually am with my beliefs.

It is a work in progress, but I'm hoping the exercise will prove worthwhile in the end. You might try it for yourself.

I believe in the God who turns up whenever and however and with whomever he wants.

I don't believe in the God who never turns up.

I don't believe in the God who always turns up.

I believe in the God who saw the children fall into the cold waters of the river in Budapest with bullets in their bodies and no shoes on their feet and did not help.

I believe in the Jesus who didn't come and heal Lazarus when he was wanted and needed by the friends he loved. He could have come, but he didn't. He could have done it remotely. He did that for others. Not this time.

I believe in the God who seems to have spoken to me.

I think I believe in the God who did something inexplicable and explosive with crucifixion and resurrection so that I can come home – and work out at last what home really means.

I believe in the God of the fog, the God in the mystery, the God in the questions, the God in Tesco.

I believe in the God who is a beggar, a starving child, a sick person, a prisoner, a lost soul.

I believe in the God who has been good enough to let me be a tiny part of healing the profound hurt in his heart, helping him to fulfil an inexpressible yearning to see his children come home.

I believe in the God who disappoints and bewilders me with echoing silence and with logical nonsenses.

I believe in the God who occasionally surprises and delights me.

I believe in the God who can bring me back to his side with one authentic, warm whisper.

I believe in the God who has been very good to me lately, in some very specific ways.

I believe with a troubled heart in the God who does not bring healing to many of the people I love.

I believe in the God who will not allow me to let him off the hook.

I believe in the God who keeps me as small change in his pocket, change that he can spend in any way he wants.

I think I believe in the God who loves his small change.

Autumn Leaves in Springtime

This was originally written, some time in advance, for the autumn 2020 issue of a magazine called Families First. *I suspect that the particularly seasonal context makes it even more relevant.*

Change happens. I might attempt to crowbar some of my familiar, reliable past into an uncertain present, but for me that process is usually not helpful.

An example. We Christians are like everyone else in the sense that we select the kind of safety that we really want. In this comparatively wealthy part of the world we enjoy great physical comfort and security, so the Spirit can blow as he jolly well listeth, but if he happens to list somewhere

where we definitely do not fancy being listed to, we can stay put. We shall still be more or less all right. Know what I mean?

What kind of safety do I want?

I need to face this question. Something has happened. The world has been gripped by a chilling wave of unease since the beginning of this year. An invisible horror crept with terrifying speed to cover the face of security, threatening to smother our capacity for maintaining the peace and safety whose source had more or less delivered in the past.

People died. People die. Numbers quoted on the news every day. Huge numbers of deaths mounting up and up. This death thing. It must be true, then. Not allowed to *not* think about it any more. It happens now. Now. Now. Right now.

That was how it was. And is.

On the day when the total number of fatalities reached twenty thousand, something seemed to shift and fall away from me. Hope. Safety. Peace. Something like that. Or perhaps it was the final remnant of belief that truly meaningful life could be found in the things of this world. Did I know that already? Yes. But not as I knew it then. I wrote these lines on that same day.

Today all metaphors of hope are neatly folded,
Tucked away for safety in a drawer.
Soon we will retrieve those silver linings,
Hope as we have always hoped before.
Even metaphors of pain and loss,
Collapse today into their cold component parts.
One survives, a wash of death and colour,
Autumn leaves in springtime break our hearts.

Now, as this article appears in the season that I love most, I am even more vividly aware that those twenty thousand autumn leaves, and all the others that have fallen since, were, by human calculations, lost at the wrong time. Families, friends and whole communities have suffered acute pain that will endure and be all the more burdensome because it is strangely trapped inside a shadow of dread.

What kind of safety do we want?

There will be many answers to that question, and all need to be heard. Within the Christian community in particular, many believers, perhaps especially those who have been forced to survive more or less on their own for months, have been trying very bravely to face the challenge presented by the effects of the virus, and the lockdown, and a general sense of puzzlement about where God was and is in the mess. I cannot help much with that problem. I have no idea myself.

I know one thing, though. Jesus said that the truth will set us free, and in my experience it can be extraordinarily refreshing to simply say things exactly as they are.

Few places, if any, are as utterly secure as a determinedly honest relationship with God.

For those who still struggle with a feeling of personal disaster, here is a prayer that might help. Change it in any way you want. Add your own truth. Have a go.

God, heavenly Father, if you are the one I hope and pray that you are, the substance of my faith seems to be collapsing. I try but fail to catch or deflect it as it falls around me. The person I find exposed by this wreckage does not impress me. Has it all gone? Have you gone? Were you there? What am I to do?

The advice from many is that, as you still love me, I must continue to have faith even when everything is cracking and breaking.

The thing is – advice from others is not the same as relationship. I cannot pretend that love fills me when it simply does not. I don't want to rely on temporary supports any more. I want something that will not fall. I want you. I want my life with you to be close and warm and genuine. I'm reaching out to you now. Meet me in my fear and disintegration and nagging sadness. I need the authentic you in a way that I don't think I ever understood before.

Thank you for listening. Thank you for Jesus. I hope that's the right thing to say. Amen.

In the last few years, Bridget and I have had opportunities to see how a change of approach or perspective can produce new confidence and security in those who want to get it right, whatever that turns out to mean.

Sometimes, though, as I have already indicated, that change might require a turning away from the path we have followed until now. Contrary to some suggestions, the entire truth is not presented to us in a single package when we become Christians. The pursuit of truth is direction rather than acquisition, and the process and progress of that direction bring us back to the Spirit and his famous habit of listing around all over the place.

What is listing? Not entirely sure, but I do intend to keep my eyes and ears and heart open so that I can be with him wherever he is. I suspect that, wherever that takes me, and whatever my fears and inadequacies, there can be no safer, more meaningfully peaceful place in which to rest.

Trouble with Whatnots

I want to thank the person who listened to one of our recordings and responded, for inspiring me into thoughts connected with one particular word that she used in her email. She might have been surprised to hear that said word was 'whatnot'. She said that in the course of looking for solutions to a particularly pressing problem through prayer, she had 'surrendered and whatnot'.

Bridget and I have spent quite a lot of time with people who have been through the rather extensive selection of whatnots that appear to be available to Christians desperate to see something happen to begin to solve the serious problems in their lives. Maybe from now on we shall ask those sufferers I mentioned, 'Have you been through the whatnots?'

I suppose we end up calling them something like this because our very reasonable passion for change leads us to try anything that might 'work'. I don't blame us.

Surely there must be a theological or spiritual button we can press that will bring the right result tumbling down, like a bar of chocolate in one of those hotel self-service cabinets?

In fact, as I am continuing to assert with tedious repetition, *nothing* works. Prayer doesn't work. Self-sacrifice doesn't work. Surrendering doesn't work. Fasting doesn't work. Giving doesn't work. There is not a single whatnot in the whole of Christendom that will work, and at this point in my life I rejoice in having understood that indisputable fact. I don't want those things to work. I really, really don't want my hard-won relationship with a God for whom I have at last managed to develop a genuine fondness to be diluted into some kind of mechanical process that might, if I apply the appropriate technique, actually work.

Bridget and I do pray a lot for everything and anything that God might be willing to intervene in. And we do make occasional sacrifices from time to time and most of the other things on that list of mine, but we know now that God does what he wants when he wants. Although we love him and have a growing level of trust in his good will for us, believing that he actually has it all in hand is really not as easy as some people seem to think it ought to be.

We also know that there is frequently a tunnel at the end of the light, and we are just beginning to know that going into the frightening darkness of that tunnel can take us to a new and much more illuminating light at the other end. Again, not easy, but some folk we know have had the good fortune to leave the god they thought they knew in the old light, only to discover in the new light something or someone much more authentic, and contained within less-limited words and concepts.

Bottom line, for me? God is heart, wisdom, silence, vulnerability and mystery. His response to us is the response of a wise father to the children he loves. The bit on prayer in Matthew 6 does not say, 'Go into your room, close the door and offer your father a selection of whatnots until you pick on the right one and he gives you what you want.' It says, 'Then your Father, who sees what is done in secret, will reward you' (Matt. 6:6).

What will that reward be? Unlikely to be a Porsche, but that is entirely up to him.

The Quartermaster's Store

This is a reply to one of the many folk who emailed us during that tense and difficult time. In a group situation, she had supported a person who was under attack, but was not sure afterwards if she had done the right thing.

I completely understand the way you are feeling over this. I am certainly not qualified to offer comprehensive or absolute truth in any of these vexed and over-discussed areas, but there are some things that might be worth saying.

First of all, whatever anyone else thinks about any aspect of the man you supported, I believe that your response was right. We are not called upon to be members of the religious police when God presents us with suffering human beings. We are called upon to listen, to offer support and to reflect the love of God. We are not allowed to judge or condemn. We are simply quartermasters employed by the Holy Spirit. The things we pass on from the divine store will have been specifically designed for the person who has been given into our care.

We might question the command we have been given in the same way that Ananias questioned God about the wisdom of making contact with an undesirable like Saul. I don't think God ever minds an honest query. Perhaps we need to become a bit more Jewish in our outlook, arguing it out by all means, but in the end we might be wise to give in and get on with it.

Of course, that responsibility carries an implicit warning. Less is almost always more when it comes to making definite statements that take us beyond what we actually know. It can be so tempting for people like you, whose hearts go out to those in pain, to give suffering folk reassurances that are fuelled more by human optimism than spiritual reality. There may come a time when we are told to speak strongly or sternly about all sorts of issues when it would be much easier and more agreeable to speak words of comfort. Love and commitment demand that we do what we see the Father doing, not what we would like him to be doing.

That, however, is a different issue from the imperative of showing care to someone who is being attacked unfairly in front of others.

If there is a God, and the evidence certainly seems to be mounting, he is active and involved in every situation involving others, whatever their history or their sexuality or their faith or their lack of faith or anything else about them. We are welcome to be involved – as long as we don't forget that he is in charge.

We are very privileged, aren't we? Lots of work and lots of adventures for us. If our intentions are embedded in the good earth of compassion, humility, obedience and an awareness that we haven't the faintest idea what God will do, it could get quite exciting.

I'm glad that chap found you beside him. Well done.

Hunger for Change

By the end of January 2021 it was tempting to dismally conclude that patience and hope were pointless. There was a restlessness, almost a sense of being caged, among the general public. The third lockdown was not the same as the other two. Certainly in this part of the world, previously unbounded energy for supporting the government and even our commitment to protecting the NHS was beginning to lose strength. People were depressed and frustrated. It had simply gone on for far too long. Rules started to be broken, especially by those for whom the natural business of living and moving forward had come to a shuddering halt. Would change happen? When?

Excuse the descent into flippancy in what follows, but I can't help thinking that the Children of Israel, after years in the desert, might have asked Aaron exactly the same questions as they waited for Moses to return from the mountain after his encounter with God.

When the people saw that Moses tarrieth so long on the mountain, they gathereth around Aaron and saith, 'Thing is, we waiteth an eternity for Moses to come back down after talking to God. He's your brother. What about an update?'

Aaron cuppeth his hand round his ear, pretending that he hath an message from Moses and God. 'Hearken now to the words of my brother Moses and the Lord your God: "Your obedience, patience and willingness to be part of our Exodus Safari are valuable to us. Please hold and we will be with you just as soon as the commandments are signed off and both tablets are fully engraved. We know you are waiting, and we thank you for agreeing to be involved in this exciting Desert Experience."'

But the Israelites crieth out against Aaron, saying, 'We waxeth bored with our not-exciting-at-all Desert Experience.

You're in charge here, mate. Giveth us something to do while we wait. Now!'

Aaron panicketh. He announceth an cookery competition offering an manna feast to the Israelite who maketh the most unusual meal made of manna. Every entry for the competition looketh and tasteth exactly the same, except for one piece of manna folded in half with a sleeping lizard inside. Aaron declareth the competition an huge success, but the crowd crieth out against him once more, saying, 'Give us something else to do right now or verily we shall smite thee with an selection of rocks and bury thee deep in an dune.'

Aaron frantically claimeth to have lots more ideas including macramé, jigsaws, face painting and making up little dances about how nice God is. None appealeth to the Israelites. Building sandcastles, going for an nice sensible walk in the sand and all other sand-related activities goeth down worst of all. Several hundred picketh up rocks.

Aaron appeareth to have an inspiration. 'An band! Let's start an musical band! Anyone any good on the shofar? No? Bells? No? Wooden clappers? Trumpets – surely! No? Lyre? Cymbal? Harp? No?'

An thousand more Israelites hefteth up rocks ready to hurl at Aaron.

Aaron quickly organiseth sundry party games. Pinneth the tail on the camel faileth owing to all camels objecting strongly to having tails pinned on them and kicking the pinners hard in sundry body parts before running off into the desert. Passeth the parcel turneth out to also be an dead loss because the parcels, made of stale manna, containeth only stale manna and, unexpectedly, the lizard from the cookery competition who sleepeth in one of the parcels. It waketh up and biteth the one who unwrappeth him. Hide and seek falleth flat because, behold, there existeth nowhere to hide and, behold, three thousand of the Israelites trieth to hide behind each other.

Then someone with an louder voice than any of the others shouteth out, 'Let's play an game called "Throw a big rock at someone called Aaron whose ideas are crap!"'

Aaron leggeth it up the mountain an little way, then suddenly turneth round and calleth out, 'Wait a minute! Wait a minute! I've got it! Everyone – giveth me all your gold earrings and, behold, I promiseth, by tomorrow, to organiseth an amazing, wondrous game that will filleth every moment of our time!'

Behold, two thousand excited mothers and daughters filleth an gigantic sack with gold, and that night Aaron sayeth dismally to his wife, 'Wife, I needeth an idea. By tomorrow. Four thousand golden earrings. What do I do with them?'

'Verily, verily,' saith his wife soothingly, 'betwixt us two I am sure we can cometh up with something that will bringeth great joy to the Israelites, to Moses and verily to the Lord God himself . . .'

Making Sense of It All?

Lockdown seemed to inspire a great deal of extra DIY improvisation. Some was very impressive. Even I decided I should have a go. Our house has three bedrooms upstairs, one quite large sitting room at the front, a smallish reception room at the back and a kitchen that works, but mainly only as a kitchen. We were definitely a study down on what we needed, but now, I am pleased to say, we have improvised.

An unexpectedly good thing has happened during the pandemic: we seem to have managed to carve out an extra area to work in. We have a large shed at the very bottom of the garden, which was intended to be a store. We have always wanted to do something useful with it. Our new plan is to use the front part of the store as a reasonably comfortable area in which to work and pray and drink whisky.

Progress has been slow, as my mobility and DIY skills, and my confidence when applying them, are all at about the same level. However, I am proud to say that I have actually assembled a very large Ikea shelving unit that covers one whole wall of the new space. Because this could only be done in the shed itself the challenge was considerable and daunting. This is how I remember the process.

I began.

It was strange. The thing spread and grew like a dumb, voracious living creature across the width of the shed floor as, pop-eyed and locked into a zombie-like state, I performed identical assembly processes as efficiently as my limited skills would allow, over and over again. Eventually, emerging from this trance, I was shocked to find myself prone on the floor, more or less trapped against the side wall. It was like some terrible slow-motion dream, or the final horrific scene from a low-budget Hitchcock film about a man who is consumed by a set of shelves.

Finally, there were no remaining dowels (wooden things you stick in holes, for those less practical than me), and it was all done, except for a quartet of very large, grown-up screws that had to be inserted into four corners in the base of the construction.

Prostrate on the crap-ridden floor in the ridiculously narrow space remaining for my body between the shelf unit and the shed wall, I remember uttering a hoarse sigh of relief as I began this final task.

The thing I had not remembered or fully realised, in the wilderness that is my DIY experience, was the likelihood that the multitude of little mistakes and misalignments that seemed irrelevant as I assembled the damn thing would come home to roost, as it were, in the struggle to achieve those four final insertions.

Resisting my actions with every fibre of its indignant being, the flawed monster that I had mindlessly created groaned, creaked, screeched and probably swore coarsely in Swedish as I battled to force it into compliance with the consequences of my myriad minor errors. It took a seriously, ridiculously, wrist-wrenchingly long time. There were at least two dark and desperate moments when the devil hissed in my ear, 'Does it really matter if the screw head is sticking out just a few teeny-weeny millimetres?' I was a wafer away from submission.

I did not submit, and, finally, it was done.

I lay motionless for a while, happy to breathe my last now that I had achieved some kind of completion. After a few hazy minutes I was struck by the thought that I might not necessarily have to actually die. I slid my contorted body painfully from its coffin, dragged myself wearily across the surface of the defeated shelf unit, and went off to find someone strong enough to help me lever the thing off the ground and stick it against the wall.

Though I say it myself, now that it's up, that shelving unit (the one that I assembled with no help from anyone else, if you remember) does look rather good.

Finally, in my experience, there is no story in this whole wide world that does not seem to be sitting up and begging like a hungry puppy to be used as a parable, a metaphor or at least a humble simile.

Very well, then. It occurs to me that any attempt to make final sense of the virus, the universe, God, us and any other related stuff is likely, in this world anyway, to make my battle with those four final screws look pathetically microscopic. If our past errors have produced profoundly faulty conclusions in the present, we shall have to leave it to God to sort it all out.

Life with No Handshakes

There came a day, about halfway through April 2021, when many of the third lockdown restrictions were lifted here in England. This new freedom was gratefully received, but for many of us any idea of celebration remained tentative. We had been through more than a year of mingled hope and disappointment. However, springtime was upon us and the vaccine roll-out was continuing its remarkable achievement of what had seemed impossible targets.

The dark cloud of fear and death remained a lurking reality, but it was good for us to take small steps into liberty, and to enjoy the sweet taste of change for the better. After watching the millionth showing of The Sound of Music *on TV one evening, I wrote the following words. By a strange coincidence, they happen to fit the tune of one of the best-known songs from that film.*

Life with no handshakes,
No hugging or kissing,
Searching my dreams
For a face that is missing,
Yearning and fear
When the telephone rings,
These are a few of our less-hopeful things.

Masks in the high street
And two-metre spacing,
Silent exchange
Of the threat we are facing,
Hushed like a choir
That no longer sings,
These are a few of our less-hopeful things.

Vaccine researchers –
Pure joy on their faces,
Springtime awaking
In people and places,
Laughter on Sundays
And children on swings,
These are a few of our more-hopeful things.

When the news bites,
When the fear stings,
When we're feeling sad,
We try to remember our more-hopeful things,
And then we don't feel – quite so bad.

7

Still Silly

Yes, still silly – after all these years.

I suppose that sounds rather shallow and undignified, doesn't it?

'Still crazy' has a much more interesting ring to it, perhaps the suggestion of a wild and romantic departure from the norm that is more truly sane than sanity itself – or something impenetrably meaningless like that.

No, being silly has its own value for me, and for most of the folk I am able to relax with. I think it might be something to do with a willingness to abdicate from any heights, imagined or otherwise, that make us giddy and foolish. A readiness to positively relish the descent into laughter and idle conjecture and, as I mentioned in my introduction, the exploration of tiny side turnings that might – and quite often do – lead us into places that we have not previously imagined. It is all of those things, and some others that I cannot quite put my finger on. A little bit of silliness has always gone a long way, as far as I am concerned. It is a reliable medicine. Now, in my eighth decade, I am serious enough about my faith to know that I need occasional doses of foolishness more than ever. Not that such doses have ever been in short supply, especially the involuntary ones. A memory springs to mind.

During a quiz, I was asked a question that was easy to answer, and I mean ridiculously easy. OK, it wasn't quite as ridiculous as 'What do you call the thing on the end of your arm with four fingers and a thumb attached?' but it was certainly right in the middle of that ballpark. I couldn't answer it. Nowadays I don't get embarrassed as much as I did in the days when I tried to exercise the talents that I admired in others but didn't actually possess. I remember this problem being excruciatingly difficult to handle on occasions. I seem to recall finding it necessary to develop a sudden acute gastric problem. To be honest, I would have preferred an acute gastric problem.

I hope you enjoy this section, but here is the question. Is it with humility, with pride or with smug tolerance that you will confess to being silly enough to join me?

While you consider that question, here is one of those tiny side turnings I mentioned.

St John of the Cross

Years ago, I tried to imagine what might have happened if St John of the Cross had been booked to speak at an afternoon Ladies Tea Club in the twentieth century. This stretch of the mind involved drawing on my fairly scant knowledge of the famous sixteenth-century Spanish mystic and my actual experience of rather unsuccessfully addressing a similar group in Sussex back in the early 1990s. Recently I turned this conjecture into a sketch or dialogue.

All you have to picture is a somewhat uncomfortable, increasingly truculent-looking man, in a long, brown, habit-like garment, standing beside the slightly over-bright president of the organisation, whose task it is to introduce *this week's special guest. It begins as the organiser is offering her speaker a little advice before he begins his talk.*

PRESIDENT: Err, word to the wise, St John – oh, do I call you St John? Or just John? Or do you prefer – Mr Cross? Or – Sinjon? Sinjon!

JOHN: Er, I really don't mind. (*shrugs*) St John is fine . . .

P: Right. Oh! Word to the wise, St John – some of our more elderly ladies will more than likely drop off after about ten minutes, or start to need the – you know – the (*almost mouthing the word*) facilities.

J: They'll need the what?

P: The facilities – you know.

J: (*puzzled pause*) Oh! Right. Right.

P: Yes, so, if you could speak up nice and loud and cheerful and keep it under fifteen minutes, that would be wonderful. And then we'll have tea. (*giggles*) To be honest, our ladies quite often look forward to the tea and cake more than the speaker.

J: Do they?

P: Yes. Unless there are slides. They like slides. (*brightly hopeful*) Are there slides?

J: Slides? No, I don't think so. No. No slides.

P: (*blankly disappointed*) Shame. They do like slides. (*bright again*) Anyway, I'll introduce you now, shall I, and we'll get going? (*taps the edge of a table*) Right, ladies, we'll make a start, shall we? Lovely to see so many of you here – twelve at a quick count, and that is very nearly thirteen. (*laughs at her little jest*) So, last time Mr Simmonds gave us a real treat with 'Slides of West Brunton as it once was'. We enjoyed that, didn't we? (*notes nodding heads*

– *whispers to St John*) They enjoyed that. The slides, you see.

J: Can we get on?

P: Yes. This month, ladies, we are very, very fortunate to have secured (*makes it sound very exciting*) St John of the Cross as our speaker! Saint John is a – let me just check (*checks notes*) – Saint John is a mytsic, and he is also—

J: (*taps her arm*) Mystic.

P: Beg pardon?

J: I am not a – whatever you said – a mytsic, I am a mystic. Mystic. I'm not a mytsic. I am a mystic.

P: Saint John is a mystic, and – ooh, now, actually, ladies, that's like that Julian who came all the way from Norwich the time before last and turned out to be a woman – did you ever?! – and told us all's well that ends well. Lovely message. Although I'd say she was a very optimistic mytsic. (*laughs delightedly at her little joke*)

J: Mystic! Mystic! She's a mystic. I'm one! She's one! I am a mystic! Listen! Listen! Myst-.

P: Myst-.

J: -ic.

P: -ic. (*St John gestures encouragingly*) Mytsic. Just my little joke! St John is a mystic, and he's going to address us on – let me just check my notes again – yes, here we are, he is going to address us on the subject of – oooh! (*with significance*) The Dark Side of the Knoll. Over to you, St John! (*she joins in the patter of applause*)

J: What! No, sorry, that's not right, is it? That's not what I said. It's not the Dark Side of the Knoll. Is it? That

sounds like – the edge of some gloomy little hummock.
It's actually the Dark Night of the Soul. Dark – Night –
of – the – Soul.

P: (*unperturbed*) Sorry, silly me. Right. St John of the Cross,
speaking to us about the Dark Side of the Soul. Over to
you . . .

J: No – no, you see, that's still wrong, isn't it? It's not the
Dark Side of the Soul. Because that wouldn't make sense.
The soul doesn't have – look, it's the Dark Night of the
Soul. It's the Dark Night! The Dark Night! It's the Dark
Night of the Soul!

P: (*wide eyed but in control – she has been an infant teacher*)
Sorree, Mister Cross. Right, ladies. Our visitor is speaking about (*enunciates clearly*) the Dark Night of the
Soul. Over to you, Saint John! (*joins in patter of applause
again*)

J: Yes, thank you. Right. My first point is that the Dark
Night of the Soul refers to the experiences of the soul on
encountering two necessary purgations—

P: (*sotto voce*) Bit more cheerful?

J: It refers to the experiences of the soul on encountering
two necessary purgations on the road to divine union.
The first purgation is of the sensory or sensitive part of
the soul, and the second is—

P: Sorry to interrupt when you're just getting into gear, St
John, but (*points*) I think Mrs Wheeler's already got a
question. (*leans forward*) Yes, dear? (*listens*) Right.
Right. Mm. Right. (*turns to St John*) So – bearing in
mind what you just said – are there slides? (*collusive
smile*) I think we know the answer to that one, don't
we?

J: Right! Let's be quite clear. There are no slides. I do not do slides. Actually, I have not the faintest idea what a slide is. I am a contemplative and mytsic who has—

P: Mystic. Mystic.

J: I am a mystic, divinely vouchsafed insight into a complex and profound phase in the development of the human soul. And I do not – repeat – I do not do *slides*! I do not know what slides are, but whatever they turn out to be, I – do – not – do – them!

P: (*dispassionately, after a pause*) Shame. They do like slides.

J: (*really annoyed*) Well, they can't have them!

P: (*brightly, after a shocked pause*) Do you know, I think we might have tea now. Let's all thank St John for his wonderful talk. (*leads clapping as before*)

J: But I've hardly begun my—

P: (*in a Margaret Thatcher voice*) Tea!!

Time for a Limerick

In my mind's eye I see the president of that Ladies Club on the evening following St John's visit. She is by the fire in her tidy sitting room, a notepad on her lap, a small glass of dry sherry in one hand, twiddling a biro between finger and thumb in the other. She has composed a limerick.

Our mystic or mytsic or myscit,
Is dry as a stale old biscuit.
The next one might dance,
Singing rude songs from France,
But on balance I don't think we'll risk it.

I Dreamed I Saw a Langoustine

Those who know me are aware that I enjoy imitating the voices of famous people. My Frank Spencer, for instance, has to be heard to be believed. When I do Billy Connolly it is as though he is present in the room. I now learn that a group who describe themselves as well-wishers have embarked on a plan to prevent me from doing my incredibly accurate what I call Bob Dylan impressions – for my own good, you understand. Well, all I can say to them is that they should go and wish well to someone else. There are Elvis impersonators who pipe up at the blink of an eye. Go and prevent one of them for their own good.

Here are two examples of my valuable work. The first is based on a Dylan song that majors on the times a-changing, or something like that. The other pays homage to his ditty about St Augustine. Mine, though, is about a langoustine. I hope you enjoy them both.

If want to actually hear me singing in the style of the great man, I feel sure the DVD is imminent.

The strepsils, they are not working
Come chemists and drug stores throughout the mall,
Those throat sweets you sold me are no good at all,
My temperature's risen as high as Nepal,
A severe influenza is lurking,
And I sound like a shovel being scraped down a wall
For the Strepsils, they are not working.

I dreamed I saw a langoustine

I dreamed I saw a langoustine,
Alive as you or me,
Scuttling through the waters,
Of this Caledonian sea.

With eyes upraised upon their stalks,
And a longing unfulfilled,
Searching for the very prawns,
That already had been grilled.

'Arise, arise,' he cried so loud,
In a voice that found no rest,
'Come all you seafood connoisseurs,
And hear my sad request.

If prawns are on your menu now,
I beg you to refrain,
The langoustine you bite tonight,
May be my Auntie Jane.'

Some Say Love

As someone who has been involved with poetry and tunes and lyrics for forty years, I may have become too aware that when it comes to writing serious songs there is a common problem. The original inspiration might be a few words that work quite well, but after that there is a whole song to be written in which the core principle has to be restated several times in slightly varying ways and expressed in rhyming verses. The need to maintain correct meter and a reasonable general level of quality would be enough to drive anyone to accountancy.

My suggestion, as illustrated in the lyrics below, is simply to allow rhyme to dictate content. The song might not make much sense, but at least you can get the job done. There's no need to write and thank me.

Some say love is a toaster,
Browning bread on both sides.
Some say love is an aeroplane,
Spraying crops with pesticides.
Some say love is like macramé,
It's made from different lengths of string.
But some say love is a clothes peg,
With a little metal spring.

Some say love is a plumber,
With a pipe wrench in his hand.
Some say love is like fruit salad,
Better fresh, too often canned.
Some say love is like a tool shed,
Filled with spades and rakes and hoes.
But we say love is a snowman,
With a carrot for his nose.

(*repeat slowly and with genuine passion*)
Yes, some say love is a tool shed,
Filled with spades and rakes (*meaningfully*) – yes, and
     with hoes!
But we know love is (*moving pause*) a snowman,
He has a carrot for his nose.

189

Moses Takes the Tablets

*Moses would definitely understand the idea of going back
to square one. We make those tedious journeys all the time.
We all do it. We set out to clean the kitchen and immediately knock a bottle of wine onto the stone floor. Fifteen or
twenty minutes later we start cleaning the kitchen.*

*You and your partner fancy a cup of tea. There's no milk.
You both suddenly know that life without tea is a life that
is not worth living. Your partner assigns you the task of
driving five miles to the nearest shop. You go there, carefully buy four items that you urgently needed but forgot to
get when you went to the shop yesterday, and drive home
– with a nagging suspicion that you've forgotten something
important. Your partner, channelling his Russian gangster
vibe, greets your return sans milk with an offer to show you
where the crayfish spend the winter.*

*Yes, journeys back to square one can be tough, especially
when, like Moses, you mess up and have to make the same,
heavily burdened, wearying trek twice down a mountain
and twice back up again.*

GOD: Moses! You're back.

MOSES: Yes, Lord, I am, as you so rightly say – back. You are
 indeed a great and gracious God who knows all things
 and sees that which is hidden from others. You are—

G: Yes, I get the picture. Actually, you coming back isn't
 hidden from me or the others. I don't need to be a God
 who knows all things to know you're back because you're
 here. I can see you. (*slightly suspiciously*) Anyway, why
 are you being so nice to me?

M: No reason, Lord, just trying to show – you know – respectful appreciation. Just being – polite.

G: Hmm. So, you got down to the bottom of the mountain, did you?

M: Oh, yes! Yes, I did. I definitely – got there.

G: Right to the bottom.

M: Yes, of course. Right to the very bottom, yes. (*mimes*) The very, very, bottom-most bottom of the lowest – bottom.

G: And you took the tablets.

M: Ha! Now, I've come up with a really funny joke about that, Lord. You see—

G: Yes, I know the joke, and it'll be no funnier in three thousand years than it is now. Stick to the point. Did you or did you not take the two tablets of stone to the bottom of the mountain?

M: Yes, I did. I did that.

G: And you held the commandments up for everyone to see as I said you should?

M: Now, here's one of those really interesting things. You know how you can make a plan, check it for problems, and it all seems just fine, and then, after all that—

G: All right, Moses, what happened?

M: I regret to say, Lord, that I er, well, there really is no other way of putting it – I broke the commandments.

G: (*puzzled pause*) What, all ten of them? You can't have. You didn't have time. You've only been gone a few hours. Are you telling me you did a murder, committed adultery, pinched stuff, worshipped an idol or two, dishonoured your parents, did something horrible to your neighbour and whatever the other four are, all in less than two hours? You must have been going some to get through that lot. I don't know whether to smite you or shake your hand. That's incredible! That's—

M: No, no, Lord! Sorry, you've got the wrong end of the staff – rod – pole –

G: Stick.

M: Stick, yes. Thank you, Lord. The stick. That's what you've got the wrong end of. I did not break all the commandments.

G: You said you did.

M: No, I didn't – well, yes, I did, but what I meant was that unfortunately – and I would like to emphasise the profoundly unfortunate nature of the occurrence – unfortunately, when I reached the very bottom of the mountain, I inadvertently dropped the two tablets of stone bearing the commandments and I am sorry to say that they were smashed into little pieces. I did have a go at sticking the bits together, but, for instance, I ended up with 'THOU SHALT' and 'COMMIT ADULTERY' with a hole in the middle where the 'NOT' was supposed to go, and I thought you might say that 'THOU SHALT COMMIT ADULTERY' sort of missed the point a bit, so then I—

G: Enough! Let me get this straight. You dropped and smashed the stone tablets on which I painstakingly spent forty days and forty nights very carefully inscribing every single letter of the ten commandments with my finger?

M: Let me think. Dropped and smashed . . . (*mutters what God has said*) Yes. Brilliantly put, Lord. That sums it up very, very well.

G: And you say you dropped them.

M: (*thoughtfully*) Well, Lord, I have to say, it is just possible, on reflection, that I may have added an in-fin-i-tes-i-mal smidgeon of extra acceleratory impetus to very slightly supplement the, er, volition of the drop.

G: (*with calm certainty*) Moses, you threw them, didn't you?

M: Well, all right, yes, I did! You see I got very, very angry because my idiot brother Aaron made a golden calf, and—

G: Stop! We'll talk about – What! What did you say Aaron made?

M: He made—

G: No! Never mind. We'll talk about what Aaron did later. Right now, Mister very, very angry Moses, there's a chisel over there. You can find two more stone tablets, just like the last ones, engrave the whole lot all over again and take them back to the bottom of the mountain.

M: Yes, of course, Lord, I'll get right on with it. It will be a – pleasure. Er. Just one out-of-the-box suggestion. Just an idea to run up and down the mountain carrying half a ton of rock, and see if it can still stand. I know you're anxious to get this done and delivered quickly. How about – and this is just a thought – it's a fair old way down the mountain, so how about if you created – a slide?!

G: A slide?

M: Yes, a slide wide enough to take me and the tablets down to the bottom. Or! Tell you what! How about a flume! I could surf down on the tablets in less than—

G: (*ominously quiet*) Moses.

M: (*worriedly*) Yes, Lord?

G: Start chiselling. And as you chisel . . .

M: Yes, Lord?

G: You just think about what you've done.

M: Yes, Lord.

8

Shadows of Shadows

I have written two Shadow Doctor *books. One is simply called* The Shadow Doctor, *and this first book was followed by a second:* Shadow Doctor: The Past Awaits. *The writing of these two novels freed me to explore the practical implications of all the stuff I think I have thought about trying to follow Jesus in the last fifty years.*

Both of the *Shadow Doctor* books are works of fiction in which the main characters are Christians. The slightly ponderous framing of the second half of that sentence reflects my reluctance to describe either of these novels as 'Christian books'. The books, important though they may seem to me, are just books, made out of paper and card and ink and whatever else goes into the manufacture of stuff for people to read. They neither offer nor possess any special power or significance or magic in themselves. They are just – books. You pick them up in a bookshop, hold them, open them, glance at a few lines, then either put them back on the shelf or go and pay good money for them. You might even read one.

Having said this, for a Christian struggling to write truth-based fiction about the lives of Christian characters, there is a major pitfall to be avoided. I refer, of course, to the temptation to assign gratuitous activities and interventions to

God himself, in order to keep the story flowing, to maintain the levels of excitement and – horror of horrors – to bring unbelieving readers to faith. Far too much storytelling about God strains to give the creator a good reference by ensuring that loose ends are neatly tied and by demonstrating that Jesus always wins. In fact, as anyone who has tried to live as an honest believer knows, flappy loose ends abound, and any clear understanding as to what Jesus himself might mean by 'winning' in specific situations is frustratingly, excitingly, intriguingly difficult to come by.

The good news for writers and speakers like myself, based on experience, is that a clearer and more impactful truth seems to emerge from openness and vulnerability than from bland theologically correct statements. The area between these two opposing trenches seems to be a no-man's-land where, to labour the Great War metaphor, change can happen – it's even possible that something as bizarre and congenial as a football match might be arranged. The undeserved kindness of God will search out any path, common or strange or occasionally bizarre, that might lead to a rewarding encounter with the hearts of individual men and women. In the final analysis, that is what these books are supposed to be about.

There are two main characters in the *Shadow Doctor* books. One is the Shadow Doctor himself, a mysterious man in his sixties who lives in a remote cottage on the edge of a forest, two or three miles away from Wadhurst in the English county of Sussex. Doc, as he is generally known, offers advice and assistance to men, women and occasionally children who are dealing with emotional or spiritual shadows in their lives. His methods are unusual, to say the least. Perhaps he is a Christian, but there are occasions when his unorthodox use of language and his attitude to the solution of problems make it difficult for the nervously orthodox to be absolutely sure.

Conscious that he has become solitary and unaccountable, the Shadow Doctor invites a young man called Jack Merton to join him in his work, but provides scant clues as to what that might actually mean or involve. Jack, now in his early thirties, has been a Christian for most of his life, and has developed a role in which he cobbles together solutions to other people's problems, mainly as a means of filling the inner spiritual vacuum that is bringing him close to despair. The cracks are beginning to show. Why on earth, he continually asks himself, would a man as deep and multilayered as Doc be interested in an empty vessel of a human being, one who is on the edge of cracking altogether?

Fascinated and intrigued by the older man's vividly variable approach to the needs of others (including Jack's own recently deceased grandmother), he surprises and frightens himself by finally agreeing to move in with the Shadow Doctor. But mysteries abound. Where did this strange man come from? What does he live on? Who is the never-present, oft-mentioned person called George? What will the future bring? Has Jack made a big mistake?

The second book in the *Shadow Doctor* series attempts to solve some of the darker mysteries about Jack's new friend and colleague. In the course of these revelations Jack witnesses and is involved in encounters that take his breath away, reduce him to tears and puzzle him deeply, as well as opening new and totally unexpected doors that may just lead to his own survival as a Christian and as a human being.

I greatly enjoyed writing those two books, and I was happy with the result. The thing I had not expected was the way in which the two main characters in the story continue to live in my mind. They have become real people, and, to be honest, I rather miss spending time with them. Like many authors, I find the fascinating thing about real characters is that you never really know how they will behave unless you write your way into finding out. Various scenarios have played themselves out in my mind. Here are some examples.

Miriam's Joke

Readers of the books who have discovered that Doc is a widower might wish that they could learn more about the woman he loved so much. Here is one tale about Miriam. Among other more serious things, it describes the birth and death of the only joke she ever made up herself.

'She loved laughing, Jack, but she wasn't really very good at telling jokes, and I can only recall her making up one in the whole time that I knew her.'

'Can you remember what it was?'

'Of course. We remember unique things, don't we? It was a terrible joke, badly told and ridiculously complicated. Actually, it happened a fortnight or so before she became ill. I think I laughed more at Miriam's single excursion into the world of joke construction than at any other joke before or since.'

'Perhaps she did it badly on purpose, just to give you a laugh.'

'Kind of you, Jack. No, I fear not. I do know that a couple of days after she first told it to me some of our close friends heard it, and would have loved to hear it again, several times over if they'd been allowed. In the end, though, Miriam put her foot down. She banned any mention of her famous joke, and that was the end of that. And it was . . . that was pretty much the end of that.'

Doc's repetition of the last phrase was spoken so quietly that Jack could hardly hear the words.

Am I allowed to hear the joke?

'Would I be allowed to hear Miriam's joke, Doc? I promise I won't laugh.'

The Shadow Doctor turned his face towards his companion, bleakness transfigured into a smile as he registered what Jack had said.

'Oh, you don't have to concern yourself about that, my friend. That is a promise you'll be able to keep without even trying. No, it's you I'm worried about. This joke can do strange things to your mind.'

Jack nodded slowly before replying.

'I'll survive. You saying that reminds me a bit of this man I used to know who'd been in the SAS. The tough-guy unit, you know. He was terrified of everything except the things normal people who are not in the SAS are terrified of. For instance, he was frightened of putting his milk in the fridge in the flat he shared because it might get nicked by his flatmates, and apart from shooting or strangling the milk thief, he hadn't the faintest idea how to deal with it. That guy wouldn't have been able to work out how to tackle Miriam's joke, but I can. Hit me with it, Doc.'

Doc scratched his head.

'You know, Jack, there are times when I simply have to accept that I really don't know you at all.' He sat up in his chair. 'OK! It happened in Yorkshire, and I have to tell you a bit of the background, otherwise the joke will make even less sense than it does when you know the context. Got it? Good.

'Miriam and I were in Yorkshire on holiday. We never tired of going up there, and one or two places became really important to us. York itself, the Dales, Otley, Ilkley, all those places. Malham Cove when we could get there, a real-life *Lord of the Rings* spot. Just about everything in and around Richmond. We loved it all. Some places were extra special, though, for slightly different reasons. One of those extra special places was a cathedral, one right on the edge of a wonderful, pocket-sized city. Ripon. You've been to Ripon, right Jack?'

Jack nodded. Ripon Cathedral was the place where the first hint of a possible change in his life had appeared. For some reason he had never completely explained this experience to Doc, and he realised now with a little shock of awareness that he had not properly made that connection for himself.

One rainy day, after a long drive to the north and a failed appointment in connection with the Bromley Church Centre where he worked, Jack had sought refuge in the cathedral on Minster Road. Jack's father had taught his son to love cathedrals.

After a dreamy circuit of the building, he had succumbed to a temptation to perform a certain, specific act for the first time. In the church circles where Jack had grown up, the lighting of candles in such a setting tended to be regarded as an unwise and inappropriate surrender to crudely visible worship or prayer aids. Nevertheless, a wordless prayer had sobbed its way out of the centre of him as he daringly lit a small candle and placed it in a holder next to others on the rack. Something unexpected happened as he studied the little flame. It was especially his. It danced and flickered and changed without reference to anything or anyone else. Uniqueness. For a few moments, the promise of liberation had filled his heart. At that point in his life, he understood neither the nature of the promise nor the need for freedom.

He found himself silently asking a question now. If he had known what the future might hold, would he have extinguished the flicker before it had a chance to become a flame? Whatever the answer to that question might be, now was not the time for sharing his memory with the Shadow Doctor.

'I've been to Ripon, yes, just the once when I was supposed to be buying stuff for the church. They cancelled the appointment. All that way north for nothing.'

'For nothing?'

Well done, Jack. Idiot. He cleared his throat.

'So, what was it that you and Miriam liked about the cathedral so much?'

The Shadow Doctor raised his eyebrows but obviously decided that Jack's uncommunicated truth could wait.

'It wasn't just the cathedral itself, although it is a magical space to spend time in. It's very good at being majestic and cosy at the same time. Not bad for a place that goes back to the seventh century. We loved it. No, it was more that we'd got into the habit of going there when we were up in the north. It was a place to sit and talk through stuff that was going on, say some prayers if we weren't sure about something that was happening in our lives – that sort of thing.'

'And that's where Miriam told her joke?'

'No, slow down. Context. We haven't got the full context yet. We're getting there.'

'Sorry.'

'No, it's fine, all will be revealed – unfortunately – when you hear the joke.'

'Right, so you went to the cathedral.'

'We went to the cathedral because both of us were – how can I put it? How would we have put it then? We were aching to give ourselves to whatever God wanted us to do for him – not quite the sort of language I would use nowadays, as you know, Jack, but that's how we felt.'

'So, you went into the cathedral to pray about it.'

Doc released a deep sigh.

'Jack, is there somewhere you have to be in a hurry, because if so, I can just – no? Oh, good. We were standing in the big open space outside the front of the building having a conversation about breakfast.'

'Breakfast?'

'Yes, breakfast. We hadn't had any, mainly because we had so enjoyed not getting up in time at our hotel, and we were trying to decide whether to go and find something to eat in Ripon before going into the cathedral to pray, or the other way round. Pay attention, Jack, this is important to the joke. We were seriously ravenous, but I think both of us knew in our hearts that we needed to get into that building before we did anything else, and talk to God. So that's what we did. We were very good. We sat in our usual place on the end of the front row of the nave, next to a big, friendly pillar, and we made a promise to God. Not something I would recommend now. It's so disappointing for him and us when we screw up. I know that for a fact. Do you want to know what we promised?'

It seemed to Jack that, quite suddenly, something different was happening. If asked, he would have said that Doc seemed to be making his own new connections, even as he followed the pathway of his memories.

'What did you promise, Doc?'

The deepest sigh of all.

'We promised, self-deluded children as we were, that we would go anywhere, do anything, and happily accept the cost of whatever it was that God wanted us to do. We didn't mean it, of course. Perhaps no one ever does. We thought we did.' He stared bleakly into the distance. 'He might have misheard. Maybe it was us who did that.' Another profound sigh. 'Anyway, by the time we left the cathedral, feeling a little bit smug, if I'm honest – quite pleased with ourselves for doing the right thing – it wasn't far off lunchtime. By now we were hungry enough to be in danger of eating each other. So we hurried back to the Sainsbury's car park, got in the car and drove twelve or thirteen miles to the town of Thirsk.'

'Where James Herriot lived.'

'Lived and worked. Exactly. We'd earmarked Thirsk for lunch when we were making plans the day before. So, half an hour later we were sitting in The Black Bull, just on the corner of the marketplace, devouring our lunch and feeling – quite good. Afterwards we ordered coffee, and I noticed that Miriam was looking kind of distracted as she sipped from her cup. After that the conversation, as far as I can recall, went like this.'

'Is this the joke coming up?'

'Yes, Jack, it is. Thanks for your patience, but I need to warn you that it seems less and less funny the closer we get to it. So, Miriam said, wide-eyed with wonder, like a poverty-stricken Victorian urchin who's discovered a sovereign in her small change and can't quite believe it, "Michael, I think I've thought of a joke – well, a sort of joke. Do you want to hear it?"

'Well, it is true that my senses were anaesthetised by a hefty meal, but I was quite intrigued as well. Miriam very rarely told other people's jokes because she was sure she'd mess them up. She was right, as it happened. But actually making one up – unheard of.

' "Yes, darling," I said, "I'm fascinated. I really would like to hear it."

' "Well, you know what happened today?"

' "Which of the things that happened today?"

' "You know – all of it. Getting up too late for breakfast, and then deciding it was right to go and pray before having a meal, and then driving to Thirsk really hungry and having a big lunch here in The Black Bull."

' "Ye-e-e-s."

' "I was thinking that God would be very pleased because we've made a whole verse from the Bible come true – well, we've rewritten it a bit."

' "We have?"

' "Yes, he must want to bless us because we were righteous when we went and prayed even though we were so hungry, and then we drove to Thirsk and had a great big meal."

' "Right, and the joke is . . .?"

' "The joke is a rewritten verse. It's from the Beatitudes. You know, the Sermon on the Mount."

' "Yes, I've heard of it, thank you very much. And the new verse is – what, exactly?"

'I remember her taking a great big breath, Jack.

'She said, "Blessed are those who hunger in Thirsk after righteousness, for they shall be filled. And we did, and we had been, and we were. Now, that's a joke, isn't it, Michael? Well, isn't it?"

'There we are. That was her joke, Jack. Do you find it funny?'

Jack scratched his head.

'Not exactly funny, Doc.' He searched for a tone. 'It's more like coming across a very small glass of tepid water after being lost in the desert for a week.'

The Shadow Doctor nodded gravely.

'She would have been so pleased to hear you say that, Jack. That is probably the highest praise her joke has ever had.'

Aelwen

I have very rarely attempted to write about romance. So much to get wrong. It scares me a little. However, it did strike me that (relatively) youthful Jack really ought to have a love interest. Accordingly, Aelwen appears in the second Shadow Doctor *book, and after quite a brief acquaintanceship the two young people become a somewhat tentative item. When Jack nervously looks up Aelwen's name online to make sure he spells it correctly, he learns that it is a Welsh name, and that it means 'fair-browed one'. He also discovers a poem*

that is simply entitled 'Aelwen'. This never made it into the
book but it might explain Jack's unusually artistic reference
to her hair.

Aelwen was the daughter of my mother's friend.
She cleaned our parlour on a Saturday while they sipped
    tea in our front room.
I loved to hear her singing as she worked.
The truth came ringing out from her,
A sweetly fashioned bell,
Nothing done by art or artefact.
Oh, that fair-browed one,
Soft hair coloured like the inside of a shell,
Was dipped in melted icebergs at her birth,
Yet not a shard of frozen ice, a speck of Eden's earth
    remained;
She was not one who tripped or fell or ran from blazing steel.
No, she was fine.
But God and mother's friend were fierce as seagulls with
    a stolen bone.
Aelwen shone like perfect, sun-kissed glass on seaside
    sand.
I listened and I gazed,
But as I dreamed of autumn walks and summer nights,
I knew with sadness and a certain strange relief
She never would be mine.

The Sieve

In the course of his relationship with the Shadow Doctor,
Jack found himself asking a lot of questions. Doc's replies

could occasionally be surprisingly simple. At other times it seemed to Jack that they pursued bewilderingly tortuous, maze-like paths towards a centre that, once he had understood it, was well worth waiting for.

In this third imaginative excursion it is mid-morning, and the two men are about to enjoy a cafetière of their beloved coffee, brought in from the kitchen by Jack. The plunger has descended, the dark mystery has been poured, and the Shadow Doctor has something to say.

'Last night, Jack, you asked me a question. Something like – how can Christians survive when life is filled with fear and confusion and there's every reason to give up altogether? Wars. Crunching recession. Pandemics. All those things. Something along those lines.'

He sipped his coffee, frowned, and set it carefully back on a coaster before continuing.

'You're still a bit short of getting the strength of this coffee exactly right, aren't you, Jack? Did you measure it out properly, or did you just chuck a random amount in the cafetière and hope for the best, like you used to before you met me?'

'Neither,' replied Jack calmly.

'Neither? Interesting.' Doc steepled his fingers thoughtfully for a moment. 'That sounds like one of the puzzles I inflict on you. You didn't in any sense measure the coffee into the cafetière?'

'No.'

'And you neither guessed nor roughly assessed the amount you put in.'

'No.'

'I see. And yet, here it is in front of us.' He looked up. 'Jack, this has got to stop. You are looking far too happy. Time to spill the beans.'

'Spill the beans – very good, Doc.'

'How did you get the coffee into the cafetière?'

'I didn't. You did. You went to make some coffee last night, but you came back after a couple of minutes and said you were too tired to bother. I agreed and we forgot about it. Five minutes ago I poured the not-quite-boiling water straight onto your perfectly measured amount of coffee grounds in the cafetière. I'm sorry if it wasn't quite to your liking.'

There was a brief silence before both men burst into laughter. Inwardly, Jack blessed the day when he had discovered that although the Shadow Doctor was almost always right, he actually seemed to quite enjoy being wrong. Jack recovered first.

'Where were we? Oh, my question last night. You never actually answered it. You went off to the kitchen to make some—'

'Yes, yes, I have completely capitulated over the coffee issue. But to be honest, there was a good reason why I didn't even attempt to answer your question before going to bed.'

'There was?'

'Yes, I was hoping that after a good night's sleep you might be happy to ask the question that really troubled you.'

The Shadow Doctor released an exaggerated sigh of enjoyment after leaning back and taking another leisurely sip of his coffee. For one stark moment, Jack wondered if the whole cafetière thing had been a deliberate ploy to allow sad little Jack a moment of relishing glory. The doubt only lasted a moment. No, that was not what Doc did. An unworthy thought. He apologised silently to God, the universe and all the fish in the deepest, darkest depths of the sea, and every one of the pelagic ones just for good measure.

But had there been a different question that he really wanted answering? Damn the man. He slapped one open hand gently against the knuckles of the other as he spoke. Don't start crying.

'OK, I suppose I was sort of generalising the particular problems I have with my own past. As a Christian, I mean. You know about all my stuff – most of it, anyway. Looking back, it was all a bit dismal, and by the time I met you it was hard to believe there was anything left. I felt like one of those old wineskins Jesus talks about. Still do feel like that, really. Dried up, and useless for putting new stuff in. I'd burst.'

'What is it you really want to know about your past, Jack?'

Jack looked around searchingly, into every corner of the room, but found nothing helpful.

'Well – was it all a waste of time? The years since I signed up. Said the prayer. You know what I mean. Faith, God, love. Have I got any of those things left in me? Were they ever there in the first place? Were there some good things? What's happened to them?' He dropped his hands to the table and leaned forward. 'Doc, you were in the shit after Miriam died. We're not much alike, you and I, but I know that happened to you, because you told me. And then you came back. How?'

The Shadow Doctor concentrated on the ceiling. A minute passed. Finally, he lowered his head and seemed to be nodding agreement with his own thoughts.

'I think that when we've finished our coffee we need to move into the kitchen. Part of the answer to your question is a culinary matter. I want to suggest a recipe to you.'

Jack smiled despite everything.

'The onion sermon again?'

'Good heavens, no. This is my own carefully devised recipe, the only one I have ever put together, and I do believe it might help.'

'This despite the fact that you can barely boil an egg.'

'Jack, my old wineskin, I am aware that there is only one real cook in this house, and I am more than happy to leave that situation unchanged. At the same time, you absolutely must try this recipe of mine. Trust me. I'm going to the kitchen now. I shall call you in a couple of minutes. Are you happy with that?

'Oui, chef,' said Jack.

It was five minutes later. Doc indicated the group of objects that he had assembled on the work surface beneath the kitchen window.

'Now, Jack, you will see that I have collected everything we need for our recipe. First of all, we have a sieve – not really large enough for our purpose, but it will do. And you will notice that I have placed a bowl underneath in order to catch everything that passes through the sieve. Next, we have—'

Jack interrupted. 'You don't seem to have any actual ingredients – things to cook.'

'On the contrary', said the older man sternly, 'we have all the ingredients we need.'

'Where?'

Doc tapped Jack's forehead with the tip of one finger.

'It's all in there,' he said. 'Shall we get on?'

Jack shrugged helplessly.

'Good! Now, next we have our excellent new blender, crucial to the success of my dish, a little china jug, and finally . . .' He lifted a fat brandy glass up towards the light from the kitchen window so that it glowed like a silver chalice. 'Finally, we have this beautiful receptacle that will contain the final fruits of our labour.'

He replaced the glass on the counter and turned. When he spoke, his voice was filled with kindness.

'Jack, I do take your question very seriously. I'm afraid – perhaps relieved – to say that I've got no platitudes for you. I'm aware that thousands of Christians, including me, have known what it means to hunt desperately for a faith that once meant everything, but for all sorts of reasons has become difficult or even impossible to get back.

'So, here's what I did. It might not work in quite the same way for you, but I can tell you one thing for sure. Whatever the Christian called Jack Merton has ended up with after all these years in his heart or gut or mind or wherever one deposits such things, is especially, unarguably, crucially his very own. All I'm saying is that, once you discover the heart of that uniqueness, you might have a place to start from. We believers spend so much of our time being told how to think and feel and behave. The knowledge I'm talking about belongs to you, to do what you like with.'

'I see – or rather, I don't think I do see. I mean – how do I do that?'

'Ah, that's where my recipe comes in. I'll take you through it, step by step, and then it's up to you to have a go if you think it might help.'

He waved a hand at the objects in front of them.

'Jack, there are no actual, physical ingredients in this recipe, because it is essentially an act of the imagination. Don't look so terrified. It will actually be quite fun when you get going. Here we go.'

He pointed at the sieve.

'So, first of all, we imagine we are filling a massive sieve. Thousands of times bigger than this. In goes the entire Bible, every single word of it, and every single thing you've ever thought about it. Bits you like, bits you don't like, bits you don't believe, bits that mean the world to you, bits you've tried to ignore. In it all goes. Every bit. Genesis to Revelation.

'Next, all the churches you've ever had anything to do with. Churches that seem to do what they should, churches that don't seem to even *want* to do what they should, and everything in between. Every Christian body that, for better or worse, has touched you. No exceptions. In they all go.

'Right, now we add every experience, from dismal rubbish to sudden ecstasy, that you've ever known, involving Christians of every shape and size, followed by every single book or vicar's letter or tract or commentary you've ever read, and a completely unedited lifetime of thinking and wondering and yearning and being excited, and failing and succeeding and feeling disappointed and relieved and depressed.

'We tip it all into that massive great sieve. Come on! Get hold of this silly little sieve, Jack. That's right. Nice firm grip. Now give the whole thing a really good shaking. Shake, shake, shake, shake, shake! All the tasteless, ugly lumps of disappointment and confusion and bad experience and anything else that won't go through the holes will just end up in the sieve and can get thrown away later. But make sure you keep it over the bowl – we don't want to lose any of the good stuff.'

He extended a hand.

'Jack, you can stop the shaking now. I think you're beginning to get the idea. Now, every single drop in the bowl needs to go into the blender. Before you turn the blender on, just use a spoon to scrape up any bits that might have got left in by accident. It all counts.

'Now, hold the lid on tight and give it a good whizz. A little longer. Excellent. Lid off. The really interesting bit. We've created a purée, Jack. But we have no idea how it tastes. Pour the liquid into that small jug, then tip a measure very carefully into the brandy glass – every drop counts, remember – and the next bit is what it's all about.

'You take a tiny, experimental sip. This will be the surviving essence of your entire Christian experience of God, church and all the etceteras, and as I said, it will be categorically your very own.'

Jack picked up the empty glass and stared at it, half hypnotised. 'So, what kind of flavours do you think I'd get?

The Shadow Doctor shook his head and smiled. 'I can only tell you about mine. Yours will be different. They'll be – yours. Mine? Well, when I did it, the distillation of my experience was definitely not bland. As far as what was left of God was concerned, I mainly detected a distinct, reminiscent flavour of kindness. Then – let me see – a fresh and attractive blend of uncompromising truth, and a slight aftertaste of smiling flexibility. There was, perhaps, even a haunting sense of what the thing we call orthodoxy might turn out to mean when it's properly understood.'

There was a pause. Jack placed the brandy glass gently down on the work surface.

'And in the end, was there some kind of flavour that was stronger than all the others?'

'Jack, I am very glad to say that the dominant flavour, the one that overpowered almost everything else, was Jesus.'

He peered through the window up towards the sky.

'So, think you might have a go on your own, Jack?'

'I enjoyed the sieve. Yes, I might . . .'

9

Love Is the Reason for Living

Some of the best and most useful gifts I have been given by a very loving God were not signed. In the case of several of these well-wrapped, anonymous treats, it was not until years later that I learned how well thought out and practical they were and continue to be. The one that taught me nearly all I need to know about the meaning of the undeserved kindness of God, or grace as it is commonly known, involved ice cream, would you believe. I was only six.

I am not a ready blusher, but a glow passes o'er my pale cheeks as I remember how swiftly I dismissed essential supplies of people and experiences because they had appeared before I had BECOME A CHRISTIAN! How could a dismal pagan past contribute anything useful to my faith-filled present and gloriously spiritual future? I really must have been insufferable.

Undeserved treats, undeserved treat-givers, undeserving treat-receivers and anyone else involved in any way and to any extent with undeserved treats are all vitally important to God, humanity and quite a lot of puppies who need to learn tricks and good behaviour.

The following story is absolutely true.

Breakfast Surprise

Have you heard of the Adirondacks? Until the middle of one November a few years ago, Bridget and I certainly hadn't. The Adirondack Mountains form a massif in North-eastern New York state, its boundaries corresponding to the perimeter of Adirondack Park, the area where we spent a brief but very warmly convivial few days with our eldest son and his wife, who were living in Brooklyn at the time. The weather was wintry in the extreme, but our rented cabin was perfect, and the hillside setting was truly beautiful. Matthew and Elena took one brief but exhilarating morning swim in the freezing waters of a lake at the bottom of our snow-covered garden. We did not. We watched them and marvelled.

Broadly speaking, all four of us enjoy variety in our lives, but there are limits. On holiday, if possible, we like our breakfasts to be prepared by the same people in the same place at roughly the same time every morning. On this occasion we were very fortunate. At the bottom of our hill, on Cemetery Road, stood the Southern Adirondack General Store & Café.

Run by Steve and Cheryl, this splendid establishment, the only one of its kind in the immediate area, was stocked with just about everything anyone might need in the way of foodstuffs, practical aids – not to mention such bizarre items as a bearskin rug that hung heavily on one wall. The café, or diner, as we seasoned American travellers call them, looked very inviting as we entered for our first morning visit, and as we seated ourselves at one of the long trestle tables, we noticed that another man was sitting at the table next to us. As we chatted to him, we learned that his name was Don, that he had been born in the area and that he expected to stay there for the rest of his life.

'So,' one of us asked, 'you've never been away from New York state?'

Don smiled and explained in his warm, gentle voice that he had been in the army for some years and in the course of his military travels had particularly enjoyed visits to England, and warm friendships formed with the people he got to know there.

It was a real pleasure to meet Don, and so good to know that his memories of our country were good ones. We turned to our satisfyingly tasty breakfasts when they arrived, and by the time we polished them off Don had slipped away.

When we asked Cheryl for our bill, she smiled and said, 'You don't have to pay anything. Don's already paid for the whole thing.'

Surprising. Charming. Faintly disturbing.

The next morning, we discovered Don sitting at a table near the door when we arrived for breakfast. Of course, we thanked him for his unexpected generosity. He simply smiled and nodded in his quiet way, and must have left soon after that, because by the time we asked Cheryl for our bill he had disappeared.

'No,' said Cheryl, 'with an even broader smile than before, 'Don's paid this one as well.'

'Well,' we replied through our smacked gobs, 'it's really, really kind of him, but tomorrow, whatever happens, we're not going to let him pay.'

We wondered what would happen the next morning. All we knew was that we had the dollars in our pockets and that our new friend was not going to deal with the check. We were determined to be tough.

'Right! Please give us the bill, Cheryl. Don is not going to have anything to do with it.'

'He doesn't need to,' smiled Cheryl, 'Steve and I are paying for your food this morning.'

We were beginning to like this part of America. The people were amazing. But the level of embarrassment was rising.

Here's a question. Would you have gone back to that diner the next morning, the last day of the holiday? We had enjoyed three free breakfasts. Could we handle a fourth? We had one more chance to actually part with some money before leaving for the city. We made a decision. We were going to do it. This time we worked out the bill for ourselves, left more than enough money on our table to cover the total and, after a brief but profound expression of gratitude to Steve and Cheryl, our kind hosts, drove away with a tinge of sadness towards another part of the state where you almost always pay for your own breakfast.

So, what was going on there? Hard to say for sure, but there is one thing that Bridget and I have learned, especially over the last couple of decades. Most people rarely find an opportunity to tell their story, and to believe that they are truly being heard. All of us genuinely warmed to Don. We love people's stories. We drink them in as travellers drink an unexpected gin and tonic in the desert. We don't have to pretend.

Perhaps Don was somehow enjoying and celebrating an inner reunion with a land he had visited and loved at a different time in his life. We shall never know. Nor will we ever know if he actually paid the third bill through Cheryl, because he knew we might not accept his gift a third time.

One thing I do know. They were lovely people. If ever you get to the Adirondacks, visit the General Store & Café on Cemetery Road. They do a wonderful breakfast.

Behind the Locked Door

Locked-room mysteries are always intriguing, aren't they? The ones that are true are especially interesting. Here is one that Bridget and I heard about recently. What do you think it might say about love?

Way up in the north of England, not far from the sea, there is an ancient and very attractive town that used to have a railway station. Back in the 1960s, a government minister by the name of Beeching famously decided to close down many of the least profitable but most charming train routes in the British Isles. One of these ran to the town in question, allowing passengers to board and alight at a station just outside the centre of town.

After the line was closed, the station buildings were locked up and offered for sale. Eventually, the redundant real estate was bought and transformed into the most amazing second-hand bookshop that I have ever seen. I could talk about this wonder for hours. Suffice it to say that the extraordinary range of books, the atmosphere of warm welcome, the readily available coffee next to an honesty box, the selection of café areas that serve excellent food and a general sense of having arrived at book heaven, make this gloriously redeemed failure one of our favourite destinations.

During one of our visits, someone who works at the bookshop told us a story. This is the tale as we heard it.

One day, someone realised that one of the small rooms in the old station remained locked, presumably since the purchase of the buildings and land decades earlier. A key that fitted the lock was finally found, and the door was opened. So exciting. What would they find inside?

There was really only one thing in the room. It was a plant. A very large plant. Growing somewhere in the area of an old fireplace, this amazing living relic must have received enough light from the skylight above, and sufficient water through a very small leak in the roof, to thrive and survive without any human help at all.

It made us think. There must be many, many Christians who have decided that passionate dreams from the past have dried up and died long ago. These dreams will be different for each person, of course. Some dreamt of using creative talents and skills. Others imagined that one day they might do wonderful things for God. Somewhere along the way those hopes were crushed. Lonely folk believed that true love would come. It has not. A few have no idea at all what love means or even looks like, and have given up the quest for understanding and fulfilment. Many followers of Jesus longed and still long to be sure that God loves them.

As a result of such disappointment, perhaps that longing may have been locked in a small room and all but forgotten.

Here is a thought. Could it be possible that God, who is not deterred by locks or barriers, has been secretly lighting and watering some of these lost dreams so that they cannot – will not – die? And if that is the case, and if by some chance we are handed a key to the chamber where our dreams remain strong and achievable, will we have the courage and the blessed foolishness to believe that, against all the odds, the best really is yet to come?

No promises, but it does happen. We have seen it happen in front of our eyes. We have known such keys take many forms. The thing all keys have in common is that they cannot open doors themselves. We have to ask for a key to be placed into our hands, and even then there is one thing left to do. It might take some courage. We must use it.

The Woods Belonged to Us

Learning how to love is an essential part of growing up. For many of us, of course, it's not confined to loving only those close to us – whether people or pets or even imaginary friends. For me, described by myself in an early poem as a small boy 'with ears that widely proclaimed a head full of emergencies', there existed a depth of passion for specific places in the countryside around the Kent village where we lived. Those cosy rural corners seemed to belong to me as much as anything I actually owned. But were the thoughts and feelings associated with those places as real and significant as I recall? Perhaps they were meaningless? If that turned out to be true, it might break my heart.

The woods belonged to us when we were small.
In early summer we were flattered
When the brand-new beech leaves came to visit,
So soft and fresh and fluttering,
Like a family of pretty girls,

Green and golden when the sun shone proudly on their
     faces.
How I wish that we could show you pictures of the places
     where we played,
Especially the camp we made – or occupied – across the
     stream,
Where some old tree had groaned and given up its point-
     less journey to the sky.
Content to die in answer to our silent prayer for some-
     where just to be.
You need no deeds or mortgages when you are less than
     ten years old,
Our latticed dwelling was a habitat, a secret, sacred home
     from home.
Older, smarter, far more foolish versions of ourselves
Would one day repossess this property of ours.
We would fancy we could see with certainty and sadness,
That mostly it had happened in our minds and waking
     dreams,
Before the spoiler leaned and hissed the lie into our hearts
That every single thing we love and lose
Was only ever made from its component parts.

I Love You to the Moon and Back

*I am crazy enough to believe that love will play the winning
hand in the end. In one sense it already has, but there is a lot
of work still to be done.*

*This crazy belief of mine, shared by many, mind you, is
a very touching, beautifully romantic notion, but I suppose
it has to be rooted in reality. A possible smidgeon of*

dialogue in our house might occur as follows. You don't fall much more heavily to earth than this.

ADRIAN: (*thoughtfully*) I've never said this to you before, but I want you to know that I love you to the moon and back.

BRIDGET: (*thoughtfully*) Good. Good. That's wonderful. Wonderful. It's Monday. Just as a matter of interest, have you put the bin out? All the recycling and the bottles for the morning?

A: (*pause*) Erm, in a sense, yes.

B: In a sense?

A: Well, in the sense that I've used all the – you know – the effort and the responsibility and the decision-making required to get the job done, but . . .

B: But what?

A: I think – now you say that, and now I think about it, I may have actually put the general non-recycling rubbish out.

B: Why?

A: (*slowly and contemplatively*) Why? Now that – that is a very good question. A very good question.

B: Right. If you really love me as much as you said, to the moon and back, could you do something for me?

A: (*worriedly*) Ye-e-es. Probably.

B: Well, on your way to the moon.

A: On my way to the—? Oh, yes. Yes.

B: Do you think you could take the recycling bin and the box of bottles and leave them outside the front door?

A: Ri-i-i-ight.

B: And then, on your return trip, just before you – you know – before you re-enter the atmosphere, as it were?

A: Ye-e-e-s.

B: Do you think you might be able to bring the general rubbish bin back and (*as to a small child*) put it in its nice plastic box in the garden?

A: Yes, yes, of course. Yes, I can do that.

B: Good. That will be one small step for a man, and one giant leap towards making sure we don't end up with a mountain of recycling.

A: Ha! Yes. Very good. Very funny.

PS, This sketch was inspired by the experience of a friend of ours, now an Anglican priest in the part of the world where we live. After her husband left her, somebody at church said, 'Well, at least God hasn't left you.'

Her reply was, 'No, but there's still no one around to take the rubbish out.'

I Think I'm Going Back

We meet and hear from quite a lot of people who speak of having experienced a tender, understandably tentative encounter with Jesus in the past. Somehow, though, that sense of new life and relationship has been lost over time. The thing almost all of these people have in common is a hope that it may be possible to return to the place where something real and wonderful happened in their lives.

There was something so good. They want to go back. I hope they will.

I think I'm going back,
To the time I learned that you could be my friend.

That time is long gone now,
But as the years go by,
The echo of that loss,
Can sometimes make me cry.
Then I have no defence against attack,
I need my friend, if he will take me back.

I think I'm coming back,
To a time when I could make it through the fear,
Yes, there were shadows then;
Sometimes I could barely see,
But as the night closed in,
You lit a path for me,
And I need you now, to light my homeward track.
I'm coming home, if you will have me back.

I think I'm coming back,
To a time when I was open, like a child.
Back then, there were days
When, for a little while,
I would close my eyes,
And I could almost see you smile.
I know now it's your smile that I lack,
So catch me please, I think I'm coming back.

Jesus loves me, this I know,
For the Bible told me so.
Jesus loves me,
Yes, he does, he loves me,
The Bible told me so.

Take It from Me

The Story of the Good Samaritan

On one occasion an expert in the law stood up to test Jesus. 'Teacher,' he asked, 'what must I do to inherit eternal life?'

'What is written in the Law?' he replied. 'How do you read it?'

He answered, ' "Love the Lord your God with all your heart and with all your soul and with all your strength and with all your mind"; and, "Love your neighbour as yourself." '

'You have answered correctly,' Jesus replied. 'Do this and you will live.'

But he wanted to justify himself, so he asked Jesus, 'And who is my neighbour?'

In reply Jesus said: 'A man was going down from Jerusalem to Jericho, when he was attacked by robbers. They stripped him of his clothes, beat him and went away, leaving him half-dead. A priest happened to be going down the same road, and when he saw the man, he passed by on the other side. So too, a Levite, when he came to the place and saw him, passed by on the other side. But a Samaritan, as he travelled, came where the man was; and when he saw him, he took pity on him. He went to him and bandaged his wounds, pouring on oil and wine. Then he put the man on his own donkey, brought him to an inn and took care of him. The next day he took out two denarii and gave them to the innkeeper. "Look after him," he said, "and

*when I return, I will reimburse you for any extra
expense you may have."*

*'Which of these three do you think was a neighbour
to the man who fell into the hands of robbers?'*

*The expert in the law replied, 'The one who had
mercy on him.'*

Jesus told him, 'Go and do likewise.'

(Luke 10:25–37)

OK. The Parable of The Good Samaritan.

When I get to heaven, it is just possible that Jesus may
have a comment or two to make about the way we profes-
sional Christians are forever messing about and fiddling
with parables that have a perfectly good, reasonably obvious lesson to teach the people who heard them two hundred
decades ago and the ones who read them now. I can almost
hear his voice. 'The thing is, my parables are not psycho-
logical novels, are they? Are they? No, they're not. They're
little stories with a simple point, rooted solidly in the world
of the folk who were the first ones to hear them. We really
do not have to wrestle, for instance, with how the return of
the prodigal son impacted on the fatted calf. He didn't
come out of it well, I grant you – but that is not the point!
Do you see what I'm saying?'

Now, of course, I don't know if he'll say that or not, but
if he does – if he does, and if he looks as if he's welcoming
a response, I shall say, 'All right, I do see what you're saying,
but I've got just three words to say to you.'

'And what are they?'

'The Good Samaritan.'

'What about The Good Samaritan?'

'Ah, I'm glad you asked me that. I shall explain.'

So, here is the explanation I shall offer, and I promise that there really, really, really – might be something to take away and think about at the end. I promise.

The Parable of The Good Samaritan has always been singularly vulnerable to a sort of possessive ownership by contrasting factions. I can remember, for instance, hearing a well-known right-wing Tory politician pointing out on the radio that it was only possible for the Samaritan to offer such abundant assistance because he was clearly involved in the kind of entrepreneurial activity that the current Conservative government was keen to foster and encourage.

Unsurprisingly, shortly after this, a representative of the Labour Shadow Cabinet expressed his long-held view that Jesus was actually using the Samaritan story to emphasise the need for wealth to be shared, and the gap between poor and rich to be closed.

I don't know much about all that stuff, but here's my point.

OK, obviously the parable has a very strong, simple message. Not easy for some of us, but simple. If someone's in trouble, you help them, whoever they are and however different they are from you. You help them. You are a neighbour to them. Right? Got it.

But here's the thing – and you probably thought of this years ago, but I've only just caught up with it – in one way the parable is also about accepting – receiving – neighbourly love and attention.

An expert in the law prompts the story by asking what he thinks is a trick question. (A quick tip. Don't ever ask God questions unless you really want an answer. Seriously.

Don't.) This is the question the man asks: 'Who is my neighbour?'

That is the question. What is the answer?

We all know the story. Bloke gets robbed and half-killed. Priest walks past, does nothing. Levite does the same. Samaritan (one of the enemy, as far as the Jews were concerned) gets stuck in and uses everything he's got to help the poor fellow.

'Right,' says Jesus to the expert in the law, 'which of the three was a neighbour to the man who got robbed and injured?'

The man can't even bring himself to let the dirty word 'Samaritan' out of his mouth. 'Well, the one who showed mercy,' he mumbles.

'Right,' says Jesus, 'you go and do the same.'

But what does that mean? If he does exactly the same as the Samaritan, he would be helping someone who's a Jew like himself. He might do that anyway, surely.

We tend to major on the clear and essential point that everyone ought to go to the aid of any person who needs help, whoever they are. Here is my question. Is Jesus suggesting something even more profoundly unacceptable to the man who challenged him? In the story, the Samaritan is the identified neighbour who brings aid, and that clear answer to the original question might well force a further ghastly thought into the Jewish scholar's mind.

Could this deluded rabbi be seriously suggesting that a man such as him should be prepared to accept help from one so alien and so disgusting?

Never! It would take some kind of miracle for that to happen.

Precisely.

As for myself, after a recent reading of the parable, I needed to give that question some very serious thought. Are there people from whom I would not wish to accept help? If there are – why not? When the very act of accepting generosity or charity would be the greatest gift I could give to someone, why do I suspect that on occasions I might want to run for cover? Why would the prospect repel or even appal me?

Don't get me wrong. I like people. I like doing things for people. I enjoy it. That's OK. But the implications of those answers I mentioned just now need to be tackled. I shall do my best.

I would be fascinated to know how others cope with this challenge. The details will be different for all of us, but one thing is for sure. We will benefit from dealing with the truth. It will eventually set us free, but the buffets involved in the process can be surprising, painful and quite scary.

The commonly understood moral of the parable remains intact, of course – but, as usual, Jesus had more than one important lesson to teach us.

More Beautiful for Dying

Resurrection happens – in many different forms.

I know someone who was frightened by autumn when he was a little boy. It was the trees that troubled him. By early November most of them looked as if they were dead, or at the very least had somehow been made to appear lost and strangely embarrassed. It was all very well for grown-ups to say that in a few months fresh greenery would once more adorn that spindly nakedness, but my friend remained agnostic about such questionable arboreal theology. Eventually, the calm persistence of nature reassured him. Spring comes back. Summer blossoms and blooms. It was all right.

Resurrection happens.

Scargill House recently celebrated its sixtieth birthday, despite the fact that just over a decade ago it closed and very nearly died. A great deal of love and the determined efforts of many, many friends and supporters ensured that, by the grace of God, new life was injected into the heart of this house on a hillside. Scargill recovered and is thriving. We are truly thankful for the chance we were given to play a tiny part in that process of rebirth.

Resurrection happens.

Sometimes fortunes change, even though the wounds are not yet healed.

Naomi, the mother-in-law of Ruth, lost the three people she loved most in the world. A husband and two sons. For the first time in her life, she knew the acid, bitter taste of emotional devastation. It was the loyalty and love of Ruth that helped bring her back to herself. A new family, a new life. The wounds were not yet healed, and the scars would ache forever, but there was a grandchild on her knee. Little Obed was a symbol of grace that she could physically embrace. For now, it was enough.

Resurrection happens. It can offer a second chance.

A man we know was approaching his eightieth birthday. Doctors told him that because of persistent heart failure he was very unlikely to reach the age of eighty-one. Yet treatment was surprisingly effective. The patient was told that he might well live another ten years. He was overjoyed.

'You know,' he said to us, 'I'm so excited that I've just faced the fact that, although I've always told people that I have a relationship with Jesus, I'm not at all sure it's true. I have been given a decade, ten whole years to explore a new closeness to the master. I'm so excited!'

New life at the age of eighty. It warmed our hearts.

Resurrection happens.

Just before Christmas in the year before this book was published, I awoke early on a Monday morning in the Intensive Care Unit of a local hospital, with no memory whatsoever of the events that had led to my admission.

I am now able to vaguely recall a visit to our local surgery on the Thursday of the previous week armed with a list, written by Bridget, detailing my recent health problems. This included several falls, increased confusion and severe headaches. According to the son who took me there, I chose to turn the presentation of my list into a sort of Lawrence Olivier-style oration. That may have been why it was not taken as seriously as it might have been.

I still remember nothing about Friday, when I apparently went for an EEG and blood pressure tests, or Saturday when I slipped and fell, or even Sunday when paramedics rushed me to A&E following a major fall, after which my brain seemed to have stopped communicating with the rest of my body. I certainly don't remember, and would rather not believe, that I decided it would be hilariously funny to declare in a broad Lancashire accent, 'I'm seventy-three, you know,' to all who passed.

Nor do I recall being transferred by ambulance to that neurological ICU for an emergency operation to deal with 'an extensive bleed on the brain'.

On that bewildering Monday morning I had not a clue where I was, and only three possibilities suggested themselves. One was that I had been abducted by aliens, probably something to do with the bright lights all around and several pairs of eyes peering intently at various parts of me.

Or perhaps I was simply in the midst of an extraordinarily vivid dream?

My third guess, believe it or not, was that God had put me in this unidentifiable situation because there was a job to be done. What that says about my view of God is quite interesting.

The truth – that someone had drilled two holes into my head to release the pressure caused by a bleed on my brain – never occurred to me. Just as well, perhaps.

Of course, my operation and that week in the ICU ward (my first ever overnight stay in any hospital) was obviously the best thing that could happen, but I have to say that it was probably one of the ghastliest experiences of my life. The confusion of that first waking was profoundly disturbing, but the nightmare did not stop there.

I was very frightened on that Monday morning by not knowing who, what or why I was.

Then, during my second night, they transported the entire hospital down to Hailsham in Sussex, where we used to live, and landed it in a field where we took a walk every now and then.

The next night they flew it back to Middlesbrough and suspended it about sixty feet higher above the ground than it had been before. These drug-induced, but impenetrably convincing, hallucinations did fade, but on the day before I was released I was moved to something called 'The Men's

Bay'. I would like it there, they said, because I would 'be with other men'. I did not like it. I found myself wondering what being a man really meant.

With absolutely no visits allowed because of Covid, emails and messages made a big difference, and the hospital staff did a wonderful job for me. I can tell you this with certainty, though: I never, ever want to go back again. I have been instructed to rest my brain. I'm trying to do just that, and I am still alive.

It was only recently, when I returned to the hospital to have a CT scan and to meet the surgeon who had supervised my operation, that I learned how close to death I had actually come. A scan taken immediately before the operation showed almost the whole of my brain squashed to one side of my skull by blood and other stuff that needed releasing. A terrible sight. My new scan, punched on to the screen with great satisfaction by the surgeon, showed everything back in its proper place.

'Now that,' he said, 'is a perfect brain.'

Resurrection happens. It can make happy-ever-after possible.

Two thousand years ago, a man sat beside a fire on the shore of an inland sea. He was cooking fish on the ends of long sticks. As he turned them slowly over the heat, his heart burned with excited expectation. A fishing boat drew close to the land. There was a shout and a splash and the sound of someone battling his way through to the shore. The man with the fish stood up beside his fire. A few minutes later, the two men had breakfast. A short, intense conversation changed a fisherman's life completely and for all time.

It had worked. Resurrection had worked.

I am so glad that the friend I mentioned earlier learned to believe in life after autumn. For me, this season is more sadly beautiful and more abundant with hope than any other time of the year. It reflects an ancient and essential promise that death – and we experience many different kinds of dying – can be an opportunity for the arrival of a bespoke variety of life that could not have been fashioned in any other way.

Some years ago, I wrote some lines about the magical powers of autumn, and about my fear that an important friendship might have been neglected and allowed to reach the point of death. I sent it with a letter to my friend, and I know you will be pleased to hear that the patient made a complete recovery. Our friendship is alive and kicking. Here is the poem.

> Autumn is a fierce reply
> To those who still deny your brooding heart.
> Flaming death in fading sun,
> The yearly mulching of elation, sadness, pain,
> A branch unclothed, the tatters flying,
> Rainbowed floating rain, tentatively lying,
> Far more beautiful for dying.
> The final breath, softly whispering, 'Enough.'
> But memories, they too come down like leaves
> On old uneven pathways.
> Such a sweetness,
> See, my breathing stands upon the air,
> And you, my oldest friend, are there.
> As evening falls, we pass between the tall park gates,

A shortcut to the town.
A shiver moves the children's swings,
The earth is soft and dark and rich,
An early Christmas cake.
We know the grass will not be cut again –
Not this year.
So down the tiled streets
The peopled rivulets,
Perhaps towards some tea.
In places that were ours but now have changed,
Though early autumn darkness,
Stares as hungrily through plate-glass windows
Velveted by bright electric embers,
We are so very glad to be there pouring tea,
Pleased that we are laughing once again,
Relieved that we are us once more.
I have been troubled by a fear that everything is gone,
The fingertips of friendship cold and numb.
But autumn is a season that returns,
With intimations of the death of pain,
And so, my friend, shall we.
Spirit, you have brooded well,
Magic, melancholy autumn beauty
And, beyond the winter, spring to come.

The Bursary Fund

Many questions about faith are not going to be answered on this side of the grave. One thing seems clear, though. We want God, and however unlikely it might seem, he wants us even more.

Some people find themselves in the wilderness of a conviction that they will never be forgiven by God.

'He knows me too well,' they say. 'He knows what I did. He knows what I didn't do. He knows how I've screwed up. He won't want me in heaven. Yes, I know all the technical stuff about repentance and resurrection and salvation, but it doesn't make any difference in my case. I'm not going to heaven.'

Here is a thought.

In common with many other Christian centres, Scargill House offers bursary funding. The bursary fund is made up of contributions by guests and is used to help those who are short of money to come and enjoy a stay at Scargill. An important aspect of this is that Scargill loses nothing. The bill gets paid. That is the purpose of the bursary scheme. There is quite a lot of money in that fund. People are very generous.

OK, so back to the 'unforgiven' folks. One of these, let's call him Raymond, comes drooping up the road towards heaven, and meets God.

'Don't bother with me, God,' he says sadly. 'You won't want me in heaven. You know all about what's inside me. I don't fit in your perfect place.'

God says, 'You're absolutely right. Spot on. You aren't good enough. You won't fit.'

George is about to turn miserably away when God speaks again.

'That's the bad news,' he says. 'The good news, Raymond, is that my dear Son Jesus, sent by me to the world, has put together a simply enormous bursary fund. Enough to pay for anything you or anyone else has ever done. I can't explain it more simply than that, but if you want to make me smile today – take the money. I want you to come home and be with me. Please take the money. Take it. Make me happy. Come home.'

Please Come Home

The words below might free us to let the love and vulner-ability of God's yearning heart speak into the depths of our own need. I hope so. When the right time comes, one simple message will ring in our ears: I love you. Please, please come home.

Please come home,
Your rooms are cleaned,
Your beds are made,
And look – empty places at my table.

Oh, you must come home,
Bring your friends,
Your families,
Your whole community, if they will only come.

Head for home,
Meet me on the road and dry my tears.
Welcome lights still burn, they always will,
Through all the weeping nights.

Almost home,
Listen for a moment, can you hear old friends and angels,
Singing in the house beyond the hill?
They sing and celebrate in hope and readiness for you.

I so want you home,
Your pain is my pain,
Beloved sons, cherished daughters,
How can heaven be heaven if you are somewhere else?
Please, when you are ready,
Come home.

My Love for You

We risk loss when we love, but knowing that is unlikely to help when it happens. Like small children surprised by darkness, we reach out frantically for something to hold on to. Some trace of what was there before the light disappeared. In the end, it might be easier to simply close our eyes and remember.

My love for you
Unique
Shape of face
Sound of steps
Tone of voice

Missing you
Us
Darkness
Confusing shots of light
Dreaming all is well
Waking
Nightmare

Searching for you
Photo

Still
In the past
Gone

Reaching for you
Warm tears
Strange hopeless hope
Hands
Arms
Empty

I loved you
So much
Love you
So much
Will love you
So very much
Always

The Heart of 1 Corinthians 13

The first book of Corinthians has acquired an iconic status in both secular and sacred worlds, particularly (for obvious reasons) in wedding services.

Nothing at all wrong with that. On the contrary, I am truly glad it happens. No, it's just that I found myself wondering what this famous anatomy of love actually means. So, beginning from the fundamental truth that God is love, I asked myself how God might have expressed his own nature expanding on the words and ideas that Paul has so carefully assembled.

Here is my stab at answering that question. For me, it is alarming and encouraging in just about equal measure. What follows is not simply a rephrasing of the thirteenth chapter of 1 Corinthians. See what you think.

Love Hurts

God Speaks from the Heart of 1 Corinthians 13

You all talk with the tongues of humankind, and some of you speak with the tongues of angels. Both of those are wonderful in their own way, but whatever tongue you use, no matter how humble or how impressive, if you don't have love, you are nothing. You are only an echoing gong. Just – a clanging cymbal. An empty noise.

Even if you have the gift of prophecy and can fathom all mysteries and all knowledge, and you have the kind of faith that can move and bring down mountains, even then, if you don't have love, what are you? Nothing. You are nothing.

Listen. If you were to give all you possess, all of it, sell the lot and give every single penny to the poor, and surrender your body to all sorts of grinding hardship so that you could enjoy the respect and admiration of others, shall I tell you what you would gain?

Nothing.

If you do all those things and do not have love, you are wasting your time. Because you gain nothing. Nothing.

So, what is love? I am love.

Love comes from me. It returns to me. It lives in me. Love is never wasted. I am never wasted.

I am love.

I am patient. I can wait. I can work. I can live – not without pain – but I can live with the grief and bewilderment of those who simply cannot see what lies at the end of the path they need to follow. They are very, very disappointed in me sometimes. I understand. I am patient. You must learn patience. Not easy, but for your own sake: you need it.

I am kind. I truly am. I invented kind. I care so much about every fascinating little nook and cranny in each and every human story. My kindness is less visible and evident than many would wish, but I actually overflow with kindness. I really do. I am kind. Try it for yourself. I will top up any lack. Then you will be wholly kind. It can work wonders. Literally.

I do not envy. All I want is for my dream to come true. All safely home. I am not happy about anyone being lost. So, I dream. I do not envy. Envy is hungry. It can consume your heart. By all means, don't hesitate to tell me what you want, but please work hard to be satisfied with what I decide to give you.

I do not boast, and I am not proud. What would that even mean? Who would I compare myself with? I created the universe. It would be utterly ridiculous for me to boast. Even so, I do hope you like and enjoy some of the stuff I have done. No, boasting would be ugly. Boasting is ugly. I do not boast, and I am not proud. Please be careful, be very careful not to advertise your virtues and achievements. It is unattractive and drains value away like stale water from a sink.

I do not dishonour others. There are some who injure and even crush other folk in this way. A few use my name when they do. They are nothing to do with me. I lift. I do not put people down. I never dishonour others. Nor should you.

I am not self-seeking. Ask the angels. Ask my Son. Ask the men who nailed him to a cross. They are here with me now. I am not self-seeking. Be the same. If you seek only for yourself, anything you gain will turn to ashes.

I am not easily angered. Whatever small groups of cross people poring over Bibles might say, I am not easily angered. There is no pleasure for me in anger, not even – especially when – it becomes necessary. Anger rarely helps. Kindness does. Patience does. Gentleness does. I can be angry, but I really am not easily angered. Ask me, and I will help to guide your anger – even make it useful – when the need arises.

I keep no record of wrongs. I could if I wanted. Of course I could. I don't want to. You are far better at doing this to yourselves and each other than I ever have been. You know, open belief in the healing of a soul can be the most powerful of self-fulfilling prophecies. Do it. I will support you. I promise you, I keep no record of wrongs. It can be difficult for you. I know that. But try to do the same.

I really do not delight in evil. I hate it. I battle with evil. It threatens to destroy the people I love. Fight it with me. Together we can attack and smash through the gates of hell. Rescue lost souls.

I rejoice with the truth. I *am* the truth. Try it. Open your mind. Taste freedom. There may be a slight bitterness at first, but in the end it is sweet and perfect, and very good for you.

Behind the scenes I always protect. You have no idea.

I always trust.

Always hope.

Always persevere.

Join me. I never fail. But here is a problem. I am afraid that the road to success can be dark and difficult. Guess what that road can look like at the worst and best of times. I shall tell you. It can look exactly like failure. Like crucifixion. Try to trust me.

Cheer up. I promise that one day things will be different. There will be no need for prophecies. They will stop. Now, there are all these different kinds of tongues. Then, you won't hear them. At the moment you know a little and you prophesy a little. When everything is worked out and completed, all the things you struggle with so much in this life will simply disappear. You will not need them. What a day that will be – for all of us.

Think about it like this. When you were a child, you talked like a child. You thought like a child. You reasoned like a child. When you become a man or a woman, you put the ways of childhood behind you.

Or here's another way to think about it. For now, you can only see something that looks rather like a misty reflection in a mirror. But then, excitingly, you and I are going to see each other face to face. Imagine that. Suddenly you will know everything, precisely as it is.

So, there we are. Never forget the three most important things. One is faith – believe in me as much as you are able. Not always easy.

The second is hope. Eyes up, and hold your nerve.

The last, the most crucial one, you already know. We're back where we started. Of course – it's love. Without love you are nothing. Without me you are nothing. Take my hand. Hang on, whatever happens. I promise to do the same. Remember that wherever and whenever you see genuine love in action, however others may insist on labelling it, you will be seeing me. Come and be love with me. I need your help. I am love. We can be love.

A Note About Love

Bearing all that in mind, you might be interested to learn that in order to check something or other in this final section, I put the word 'love' into the search engine for the entire book. My laptop produced the following response:

There are too many results to show here.

I'm so pleased that my new book is filled with love.

Epilogue

I was allowed to live through that operation of mine. Why? I have no idea. I can think of other people whose much more useful lives have been cut short by death. Perhaps there is something left for me to do. I hope so. It might be something very small. That would be fine. No less puzzling, but absolutely fine. God seems so strange sometimes.

You are particular

You are particular in your interventions.
No, not picky,
Just – particular.
You are all loving,
And all powerful.
Because you are particular, this winds up a paradox
That ticks and tocks from far too many clocks
Through every hour I spend with you.
However, despite this and all other paradoxes, I'm hang-
   ing on,
I am content, like your friend John,
To be small change in your back pocket.
Spend me as you wish, feel free,
But please do register my humility.
In this respect

You will have noticed, I expect,
My gift for subtle self-advertisement.
I repent.
I did abstain for half of one whole Lent,
But then up popped a tempting situation,
A chance to rise in someone's estimation.
I enjoyed the moment, but quite soon, as all such
    moments must,
It turned to dust.
Now, don't go all Old Testament on me,
All OTTOT.
I live with endless mysteries, the paradoxes,
The infernal ticks and tocks from those imaginary clocks.
Find the Great High Priest;
If he's free, I think he'll do his little laugh
And say a word on my behalf.
You can't roll Hebrews in a ball and consign it to the bin
It's in.
I know you are omnipotent,
But when it comes to changing what you've promised,
Even you can't win,
Can you?
Is that a paradox?
Listen, though, here's a thing,
I've got a song for us to sing.
Creationists won't like it,
But then – they don't seem all that keen on anything.
You'll know the tune.
The words are changed a bit,
It might be heaven's next enormous hit,
Who knows?

Ask the angels.
This is how it goes

Charlie is my Darwin,
My Darwin,
My Darwin,
Charlie is my Darwin.
The not so young, heavily bearded, early and significant
  contributor to the science of evolution.

There we are then, that's my contribution,
A silly song, a joke or two.
Meanwhile,
What do you do?
You control the universe, the passage of the spheres.
You know the joy of hearts remade and rescued through
  two thousand years.
You field the disappointment, the billion, multi-trillion
  cries of pain, the floods of hopeless tears.
But as you wait and long with all your heart for Earth
  and Heaven to be reborn and made to shine and all
  that grand important stuff,
We meet from time to time – don't we – you and I?
For just a little while,
And when we do, you must admit, I sometimes make you
  smile.

HODDER &
STOUGHTON

Hodder & Stoughton is the UK's
leading Christian publisher,
with a wide range of books from
the bestselling authors in the UK
and around the world ranging from
Christian lifestyle and theology to
apologetics, testimony and fiction.
We also publish the world's
most popular Bible translation
in modern English, the New
International Version, renowned
for its accuracy and readability.

Hodderfaith.com   Hodderbibles.co.uk
 @HodderFaith    /HodderFaith